WHILE SHE *sleeps*

DANI RENÉ

PLAYLIST

Ride - SoMo

Shameless - The Weeknd

Scars to your Beautiful - Alessia Cara

Breathe - Fleurie

I Mean It - G-Eazy, Remo

Soldier - Fleurie

Don't Deserve You - Plumb

Echo - Jason Walker

My Hell - Aaron Richards, GLXYFX

Fine the full playlist on Spotify

While She Sleeps

Dangerous. Unstable. Obsessive.

She believes in fairytales and awaits her prince.
But I arrive at her doorstep and I'm far from royalty.

*The shiver down my back tells me he's there. As if he were
touching me. Cold, angry, aloof—he's everything I don't need.
But I can't turn off my attraction when he's near.*

My sleeping beauty doesn't realize just how dangerous I
am. She trusts so easily, smiles so beautifully. And while
she sleeps, I watch. With each passing night, I become
more addicted.
Until I'm a man obsessed.

*I feel his gaze on me, watching while I sleep.
He pushes me away in the light, but in the dark, he comes to
me like a moth to a flame. I crave it. He doesn't know just how
broken I am.*

I believed she was the light to my darkness.
But it turns out my sleeping beauty likes to dive into
the shadows alongside me. She's mine, but that decision
could kill us both.

Dedication

To my Deviants who love the bad boy who does all those dirty things that make your toes curl and your body tremble. ;)

PROLOGUE
Vera

Hᴇ ɪs ᴛʜᴇ ғɪʀsᴛ ᴘᴇʀsᴏɴ ᴡʜᴏ sᴇᴇs ᴛʜᴇ ʀᴇᴀʟ me.

Sees what's hidden inside.

Not the darkness, not the light, but the gray in between.

I was the first person to see past his affliction, and that's what started our twisted journey. We were both broken by the life given to us, and in order to survive, we needed each other.

I spent my life falling in love with the stories my nanny read to me. The fairy tales that spoke of princes and castles. And since I lived in a castle—well, a house so big it could be considered a castle—myself, I always thought I would find my prince.

I lost my mother when I was young. And when I fell into the darkness of my depression, I found solace in the depravity that came with addiction. I didn't waste away on drugs, and I certainly didn't drink myself into a coma.

No.

My need came from something far dirtier and unmentionable. A desire that grabbed hold of me and didn't let go.

Until him.

My life was always filled with light, until my mother was no longer around, and I was left to my own devices. Children shouldn't be left to fend for themselves, especially children like me—privileged. I admit I'm broken, that I should never have found myself on the website I had become addicted to.

But that same lapse in judgment brought him to me.

Each night, I would wait and watch the screen as it illuminated my old bedroom, and I would watch for him. My heart would kick wildly in my chest when I saw his name light up, and his message appear.

I don't have anyone else but him.

I'm the possession of someone who ran away from me when I first met him. The memory is still clear of that day, and I recall his disdain for me so clearly. But now I find myself in the dark in a bedroom, which is homely, warm, and cozy. I've fought, screamed, and cried, but my owner only ignores me when I act like this. He may have shown me his face, but I've yet to see his soul.

For now, I wait. I *know* he's there, watching.

I don't know how long it's been.

Only that he visits me every day.

I know his name. He was the first person I ever came to love and to crave. And even now, I know he will be the only one who understands my desires.

He makes me feel things.

I shiver again when I think about him. Rolling onto my back, I sigh loudly, and it echoes in the vast bedroom. It's different from the one I had while I was growing up.

I no longer have teddy bears on my bed. There are no longer pink and pastel blue furnishings and curtains. This bedroom is filled with deep shades of cobalt and charcoal hues that offer more warmth than what I'd envisioned.

Each night, in the dark, my visitor comes to me. He talks to me in that deep, gravelly tone, which only turns the spark inside me into a raging inferno. He tells me he's ill and that he doesn't understand why he is broken.

I want to tell him I am too. My heart, my mind, it's not the same, and there's nothing I can do about it but tamp it down and ignore it. I want to ask him so many questions that plague me daily, but I don't. Perhaps the less I know, the better.

The sun streams through the window, informing me of a new day. He told me I'll be able to go outside soon. And I can't wait to run through the forest. I've sat in the window seat every day since I woke up in this bedroom, and I've watched the birds flit about and the flowers bloom as spring nears.

Last night, he came to me and sat for a long while, just talking. I want to see him, to ask him why he's taken me, brought me to this place that doesn't seem like a prison, but sort of is. It's a cabin, hidden amongst tall trees and green grass.

I'm thankful he's been kind to me, not hurting me in any way. I imagine other girls who've been in similar situations, may not have been as lucky as I am.

My body trembles when I hear the lock of the bedroom door clicking, and I realize he's bringing in the tray with food for me to devour. He feeds me, keeps me hydrated, allows me all those normal comforts; the only thing he doesn't give me is his truth. But soon, I know he will.

The spicy scent of his cologne still hangs heavily in the room from last night, and I'm filled with want for him to stay here with me. He makes me crave the nearness of him. I watch as he sets the tray on the vanity before he disappears again.

How can I want him when he hides from me?
How can I need him when he won't let me in?

CHAPTER ONE

Logan

One week ago

I CLICK ON THE PROFILE, READING THE NAME *Sleeping Beauty* before scanning her bio. It's short and sweet, just like I imagine her to be. I shouldn't do this, but I can't stop myself. I found out how broken I was when I turned seventeen and found myself needing release while I watched my girlfriend at the time asleep beside me. We had been studying late into the night, and while she slept, I found more pleasure than I ever had.

The moment I came all over my hand, I rushed to the bathroom, cleaned up, and left. I never once went back to her house. Fear held me hostage, keeping me from even talking to her, telling her what I did.

I spent my nights searching for reasons why. But nothing could stop it, I was broken. My desires ran deep into my veins. And I couldn't tell anyone about it. The secret was mine to bear, and I had to do it alone.

For the first time in years after that incident, I met someone else. She was kinky, she would let me tie her up, blindfold her, and for a while, it worked. But happiness doesn't last forever.

I realized I was never going to be with anyone long-term when I woke my ex-fiancée while I was jerking off over her sleeping form. She looked so beautiful, peaceful and unaware of my perversions. I hid it from her for two long years. But the moment she opened her eyes and felt the hot mess I'd made all over her chest, I knew I needed to leave.

To run so far away, nobody would ever be subject to my sick desires.

I couldn't explain it away, and telling someone on the first date that you can't get hard unless she's asleep isn't something you want them to know. And that's why I find myself here, on the dark web, where I can find those who are broken—just like me.

I open her photo, which is blurry at best, but I can make out her bra, a soft-pink color, and the panties she's wearing match. I open the messenger app and type out my first contact with her.

Logan: Are you looking for a Prince or just another bad boy who can fulfill your fantasies?

I don't know why I'm doing this, but it's the safest way to find release. It's the only way. I glance outside. The moon hangs in the sky, heavy and bright. The cabin I bought is secluded, away from prying eyes, because the moment I'm surrounded by people, I feel my anxiety twisting inside my gut, hammering against my chest. Reminding me that I'm nothing more than a monster.

Her reply dings from the speakers of my computer, and I'm too afraid to open it. This is ridiculous. It's not like she's here. And if she were, I doubt she'd stick around long enough to know who I am.

SB: I learned a while ago that princes aren't as charming as they claim to be. At least a bad boy doesn't apologize for his behavior.

I chuckle. She's cute.

Logan: This is true. But what if the bad boy was dangerous as well?

SB: Then, I suppose it would be even more exhilarating. Wouldn't it?

She's challenging me to see if I'm said bad, dangerous boy. But what she doesn't know is I'm a man, nearing my thirties, and she's only twenty years old. I should shut this down, stop responding, but my fingers have a mind of their own.

Logan: It would be. Danger excites you. Doesn't it?

SB: It does. I don't know why. Perhaps I'm

broken in some way. Maybe I'm meant to be the bad girl who corrupts the good boy.

I can't stop smiling. I sit back, watching the screen as if it's meant to give me answers. Do I tell her who I am? No. If I do, she'll stop talking to me. I keep my gaze pinned on the screen, and then I see another notification pop up.

SB: *So . . . your profile doesn't tell me what it is you're into.*

Logan: *I know. I . . . I don't know how to tell people about it. It's not . . . normal.*

I sigh as I push off the bed and make my way into the kitchen. I don't want to see her response. But I also do. The forum we're on isn't exactly *normal,* and she should expect chat partners to ask for random shit, and mine isn't as bad as some I've come across, but it doesn't mean it won't scare her off.

Sleeping Beauty.

How is it a girl would want to be a fairytale character? Brought up on stories of happily ever after isn't the right way to live. I should know. I tap my phone screen and see a message from my mother. My father would never contact me, but she does.

I know she misses me. She wants me to return home, but I can't. After the darkness I brought on the family name, my father would sooner disown me than have me back in the house.

My computer dings from the bedroom, but I ignore it for a little while. My mind is on my folks for the moment, and I consider responding to my mother, but after a moment, I turn and head back to the bedroom with a bottle of beer.

I flop on the mattress and tug the laptop toward me. Waiting for me are two messages from the little princess. She's not even seen what life can do, and she's on this fucking website, talking to me—a stranger. At least, that's what she thinks.

What the hell could've happened to her to push her into this life?

Onto this website?

SB: Normal is subjective. Perhaps you should

just come right out and say it.

SB: But if you'd rather not, I won't pursue it. I'm into . . . I need . . . I like being watched. Is that wrong? I mean, the fear that courses through my veins spark my arousal, and then I'm lost to it until I find release.

I stare at the screen. I read her words, then reread them. I try to make sense of her. In just that one confession, she's given me more than I could ever have hoped to give anyone in my own damn life.

She deserves an answer. She should get one, but I can't bring myself to do it. My fingers hover over the keys as I regard her name. I know it's not real, but just the thought of her being able to accept my ache, to see her unconscious, to feel her limp body as I curl myself around her and rub my cock against her smooth, porcelain flesh, has me groaning.

SB: I like when a man . . . I enjoy a man to hunger for me. I crave attention, the need to feel his eyes eating me up. I know it's dangerous, but this is how I find my fix. By roleplaying scenes online, so

I don't do it in person. Is that why you're here too?

Fuck.
My fingers move without me thinking.

Logan: Yes. Your needs and my desires seem to tie into each other more than I could've hoped for. But this is all it will ever be, my beauty.

SB: I didn't ask for more. Did I?

She's right. She didn't, and I'm assuming she'd ever want to see who I am. The moment her gaze landed on my face, she'd know why I'm hidden in the middle of nowhere. Why I'm living in a small town in the corner of the world where nobody will find me. Where nobody can recognize me.

I consider my next response. Do I tell her more? *Can* I tell her more? Of course, I can. But I'm still afraid. Being shunned for something I have no control over has put fear inside me, and every time I have a glimmer of hope that sparks within me, it's extinguished before I have time to really and truly feel it.

Logan: Then why don't we get to know each other? Tell me about your favorite role.

I wait.

Five minutes pass and nothing, yet her green light still shows she's online. So, I haven't scared her off just yet. That's a good thing. But waiting for a response is like being hanged by the fucking balls—painful, excruciating.

SB: I'd like to feel like I've lost all control. Like I'm nothing more than a rag doll. Lying on a surface of your choosing. I want to have a video recorder on me, to show me what you've done to me after. I want to feel the ache of you inside me when I wake up. I want you to hold me down, keep me there until you've had your fill of me. And when you're done, I want to wake up with the scent of you on my skin.

Jesus fucking Christ.

I have no response to that. My cock is throbbing so hard I can't think straight. All I can envision is her, lying on that pretty pink bed while I enjoy her body just like she wants. While

CHAPTER TWO
Vera

THE GRAY BUTTON GLARES AT ME. HIS FINAL words to me hit me right in the chest. I was enjoying the banter, the back and forth, but it seems I've scared him away. I allow my eyes to take in his last message once more and try to figure out what it means.

BP: I'm no good. Not at all. I don't want to hurt you.

It doesn't make sense. His screen name—Broken Prince—screams to me, begging me to hang on. To give him time, but I don't think he's going to come back online tonight, or perhaps ever.

Sighing, I lie back on my bed and stare at the ceiling. The light of the computer goes out when I close my laptop, and I'm left in the soft glow of the full moon, which peeks through my window like a voyeur. It watches me every night, waiting, biding its time, just like the darkness I seem to have awoken inside me.

I didn't lie to him. I do want those things. I read about them, fantasize about them daily. It's a scary thought needing such depravity to find pleasure. Guilt weighs on me, dragging me into the darkness I can never relent from because it's part of me.

I have classes in the morning. Since I'm studying correspondence, I'm allowed to do it from home, or a coffee shop, or anywhere really, and I enjoy not being around crowds of people. When I was forced to leave the city, to find somewhere less conspicuous, I did my research and packed my bags.

I wonder where *he* lives. The broken prince. It's heartbreaking to think he's alone in the darkness, perhaps even staring up at the moon like I am right now. I didn't ask him if he's in the States, or if he's internationally based, but I guess it doesn't matter.

Maybe if I knew he was closer, it would make this more *real.*

It's best I don't.

I roll over, facing the window, allowing my eyes to flutter closed. Weariness hits me hard, and yet, the ache between my legs is still there. Ever present. Tears burn the backs of my eyelids as I try to focus on the sky, stars, and moon. It's been like this for so long it's become a part of who I am.

My hand finds the apex between my thighs, and I touch my center. Immediately, the need burns like fire racing through my veins. My blood heats, and I close my eyes, picturing *him* in my mind, even though I have no clue what he looks like.

I roll onto my stomach, shoving my pillow between my legs, and I roll my hips. I whimper and moan, the sounds soft, yet they bounce off the walls in the darkness, and I feel that familiar lust that drives me to imagine a more dangerous scenario.

Would he pin me down?

Would he hiss in my ear?

Would he choke me until I pass out?

My body shudders, and pleasure shoots through me from the top of my head to the tips of my toes. I tremble as I come down from the high and feel my panties now soaked through.

The scent of sex, of desire, hangs in the air, and I open my laptop before I have time to rethink it.

Vera: *You can't just tell me that and then leave. I thought . . . I figured you had needs like I do. Can we start over? Would you listen to me while I talk to you over a voice chat? Can we go back to the beginning before I told you my fantasies?*
SB

Then I shut my computer and roll over, allowing my sated body to fall asleep with dreams of a prince who can take me away and offer me the forever I've been waiting for.

My alarm wakes me at seven, forcing me to roll over and slap my hand over the iPhone screen to shut the damn thing up. I'm still tired when I think about what happened last night, and then it hits me—I messaged him back.

Shit.

Pushing my comforter down, I swing my legs over the edge of the bed and pull my laptop up before opening it. I log in, and the browser refreshes. Sadly, there's no response, and the ache in my chest is a reminder of my stupidity. Why did I think he'd want what I do? I don't know why I feel so sad about it. I don't even know him, but when you find a soul that speaks to yours, you make haste to grab at it.

But I think I did it too quickly, and I lost sight of taking it slow. Perhaps it shows my immaturity. Instead of wallowing in my thoughts, I head to the kitchen and grab a mug from the cabinet before setting it under the Keurig. I push the button, leaving it to do its thing.

In the bathroom, I open the tap, washing my hands before grabbing my face wash and squirting a dollop in my left palm. I lather it up before running my hands over my face. Refreshing and cool, the cucumber scent is fragranced over my hands, and I inhale slowly, hoping it will calm my erratic thoughts.

Once I'm freshened up, I grab my now-full mug and settle on the sofa with my laptop and notebook. I have one assignment to finish today before I can go out for a run. It's one of the only activities I enjoy because it allows me to forget the world and focus on my breathing.

The click of the keys is calming as I work. Time passes, and when my stomach grumbles, I glance at the clock, noting it's nearly midday. Sighing, I set my computer on the table and stand, stretching my arms above my head. Perhaps it's time for that run now.

I quickly change in the bedroom and grab my phone and keys, along with my air pods, which I push into my ears and find the playlist I usually run to.

I hit the street. There's a lunch rush, and I duck down the road and toward the park where there's a thick crop of trees. The path is clear. The music captures my attention, and I allow my mind to drift away.

As I wind through the thick trunks of the oaks, I smile at the smell of fresh rain now slowly trickling from the clouds hanging overhead. Even though I grew up in a bustling city, I love living in Pine Lake. There's nothing like the fresh country air and the softness of the land compared to the concrete jungle I grew up in.

When I moved out here, I didn't expect to love it so much. But as time passed, I found myself falling more in love with the town than ever before. Now I can't see myself living anywhere else. I take a left and suddenly stop. My body stills, and I pause the music to listen. My ears prick, and a cold shiver races down my spine.

It's strange, but it feels as if someone is watching me. I spin around, my eyes raking along the path between each of the tree trunks, but I don't see anyone. The hairs on the back of my neck stand on end, and I shiver even though I'm sweating.

I'm not sure how long I've been running, but it doesn't feel long at all. When the feeling passes, I flick the music back on and decide to head home. It could be nothing. It could just be my mind playing tricks on me.

Being on the run for so long, I've learned to

be wary, walking on the main street, especially when I'm on my own. But this felt like more than that. I really am convinced I felt someone behind me.

Shaking my head, I make my way out of the other end of the small wood and come out onto the main street, which leads to the apartment block I live in. Pine Lake has a population of a few thousand people. With two hotels and a few bars and restaurants, it's not the tourist trap that most small towns can be when they're famous for something in particular.

Thankfully, it's not *that* small where everyone knows your name and your business. And even though I may recognize some of the residents I see every day, they're all focused on their own lives rather than that of their neighbors.

When I reach my apartment door, I see a small package sitting on the welcome mat. Once again, a cold shiver trickles down my back, but I put it off as just the sweat from my run. When I pick up the small box, I notice the card on top. There's an unfamiliar scrawl of two letters in black that steals my breath.

S.B.

I spin around again, even though I know there's nobody behind me. My neighbors' door is closed, and their dog isn't barking like he normally does when I'm on the landing, so I presume they've taken him for a walk.

I unlock the door and go inside before kicking it shut behind me. Dropping my keys in the bowl on the table at the entrance of my apartment, I pick at the ribbon on the box and lift the lid.

Inside, on a silky cushion, sits a gold bracelet with a rose pendant. *What the hell?* The card doesn't have anything more than the initials on the front. This doesn't make sense. If it was *him,* it would be weird, because how would he know where I live?

Setting the gift on the coffee table, I grab my laptop and open the lid. While I wait for it to boot, I grab a bottle of water from the fridge and flop onto the sofa. Once I'm logged in, I open the browser and the website where I was chatting to the stranger last night.

There's still no response from him, but I decide to make it known that I'm freaked the hell out.

After I hit send, I pick up the bracelet again. I must admit it's beautiful. The golden chain is delicate and lovely, and the rose is so realistic. I can't help but smile, even as fear twists in my gut.

I'm always careful when I log onto the web. I make sure I use a VPN and never give out information about who I am, or even my real name. I've seen far too many reality shows where girls are kidnapped, stolen from their homes because they gave out far too much personal information to a stranger online.

That's not me.

I'm not stupid. I know the risks I took by signing up on that site. *Anonymous Meet-Ups* was nothing more than me quelling the need for company. And I've never even had the courage to meet anyone from there.

As my gut churns with nerves, I wait for the ding to come through. But he doesn't respond. I make coffee. I can't eat lunch because my nerves have gotten hold of me, twisting in my gut, and all the while, nothing. While I attempt to work on my assignment, the bracelet lies on the table, glaring at me with accusations I feel right down to my core.

Can it really be him?

Or am I losing my mind?

CHAPTER THREE
Logan

She's so beautiful. More so than I ever thought possible. When she runs, she's exquisite, like a gazelle, appealing to my beast that's beating down the caged door I've kept him in for so long. A temptation. I didn't think I would come here. When my contact gave me the details after he searched for her, I stared at them for so long. Realizing I lived merely five hours away shocked me. We were so close, practically neighbors and I didn't know.

I waited two long years to finally see her again. But today, I couldn't stifle my need for her anymore. I got in the car and drove all night until I stopped at the small coffee shop in town.

I waited. I watched. And then she appeared.

Amongst the trees, she reminds me of a princess lost in the woods, seeking the wolf. *Would she be afraid if she knew I was right here?* I haven't checked the website today, but now that I'm in my hotel room, I open my laptop and log into the Wi-Fi before opening the browser.

The message alerts come through the moment I'm on. Two from her. I read both, twice, then a third time to make sure I've read them correctly. She got my gift, but she also told me she wanted to start over. I'm not sure why she would feel the need to say that.

I wonder how to proceed. *Do I tell her I'm here? That I'm watching her?* No. That's creepy like she said in her message. But she doesn't understand how much I needed to know her. Even if it's from afar.

I can live with that. Perhaps I should leave. But even as I think it, I know I won't. I can't. Not yet. Sighing, I hover my fingers over the keyboard and smile when I type out my response.

Logan: *I must apologize for scaring you. I didn't mean to. My . . . work . . . allows me certain perks,* *and finding people is one of them. Like I found you. I'm not going to make contact with you again until you ask me to. But I needed you to have the rose, just like Sleeping Beauty did in the story as she slept. I'm not right as I told you, and the conventional ways of doing things don't really appeal to me. So, I have my own way. I hope I haven't truly scared you off. If I have, I wish you well. My Beauty.*

I hit send and shut the laptop before I can go back and send her more messages. I shouldn't have come here. My mind is a mess of thoughts that seem to all dance together, making life more difficult and painful to deal with.

My phone vibrates, and I know it's my mother checking up on me again. I haven't responded to her in two weeks; surely, she's gotten the hint by now. I can't go home, and I can't communicate with her. My father would be watching all messages, emails, and calls that come through. And I can't put her in any danger.

Shutting my phone off, I grab my keys and wallet and head downstairs. On the street, I turn left instead of right, because I know if I do, I'll end up outside her door. As much as I'd love to see her in person, face-to-face, and allow her to look at me, to see me, I can't.

Not yet.

Not until she's replies and tells me to come to her.

The town is pretty enough, with shops, cafés, and even a small bookstore, where I duck in and get out of the cool breeze and rain that's suddenly started pelting down. The lady behind the desk smiles, and I offer her a nod. Most people in such a small, far-off town won't recognize me, and I'm thankful that my beauty doesn't live in a city where my father's influence can be felt for miles.

Being the son of an influential family in this country had its perks, but I walked out of that life. I don't ever want to go back. Since the moment I stepped foot out of the mansion, my father's blood money built; I'm no longer considered his son.

Herbert Phillip Oakridge—otherwise known as King of Chicago by running his own import and export business and playing the stock market; he's built an empire. Years have gone by, and my father has embezzled millions, yet the police turn a blind eye.

Thankfully, Daddy's influence has allowed me perks and being able to seek out this beautiful stranger, this princess, has been one of the more positive things I've done using his contacts.

My father may share my name, or I share his, but deep down, he would pull the trigger himself if he knew I was doing this shit again. He's allowed me certain freedoms, but I have a feeling if he were to find me, I wouldn't survive walking away from him. Which means I need to be more secretive about my actions.

I close my eyes and think back to only a few hours ago, reminded of her beauty. Even though it's not visible in her profile photo on the website, I can now recall her lithe, slightly curvy figure as she ran through the woods. It's been a long while since I've felt this connection. And I know I can't let it pass.

I will make her mine.

One way or another.

I'll ensure she's in my arms, in my bed, and I won't let her go. I pick up a book from the shelf and scan the back of it, but my mind is not focused when the bell above the door chimes.

It's been a long while since I've been around so many people at once. My cabin is quiet. And I enjoy the silence, more so than the ramblings of strangers.

"Hi, how are you?" The soft, melodic voice stills me. My heart hammers against my rib cage, and I hold my breath, waiting for more of her voice. I know it's her. Somehow, I can *feel* her.

"I'm doing all right, darling. What can I do for you today?" the older lady asks her with a smile, hinting in her tone.

"I'm looking for anything dark and foreboding. Like crime thrillers?"

"Ah, I have a few that came in today. Follow me." They move through the store, and I cast a glance over my shoulder to see her long, dark hair hanging to the middle of her back. She looks like she's just had a shower, possibly after her run. My gaze trails down her body, and that's when I see it — the bracelet.

Surely, she must know that if I'm in town, and perhaps walking around the streets, I could bump into her and see it. *Is it a sign that she wants this as well?* I haven't checked my messages, and I left my phone at the hotel. I can't even log in to see if she's replied to what I asked of her.

The women are hidden by a bookshelf, and I make my escape, racing through the wet streets back to my room. My chest is tight with anxiety. I wonder if she is considering being mine. *Would she?* If she knew who I was. Or would that change her mind about me completely? Without both our fathers getting involved again, perhaps there's hope. But I can't show her who I am yet.

Not yet.

When I laid my eyes on her, I was livid my father expected me to be happy about his choice. At the time, she was nothing more than a child. I think back to the day I first saw her.

"This is Vera Rose," my father tells me. My disgust is evident on my face as I regard my father. The girl before me is not even a teen yet. We've just bombarded her tenth birthday. She smiles up at me, unsure why we're looking at her.

Stephen looks at his best friend, my father, and smiles. They've arranged this, and I'm about to refuse their plans. My father expects me to want this . . . girl?

"No." I turn on my heel and head back to the front garden and out to where the car is parked in the enormous driveway. It snakes around a fountain of two angels fighting over a water jar.

"Logan." My father's voice halts me for a moment, and I know he's angry, but I don't care. This is ridiculous. How can he think I would want her? "When she's eighteen, she'll be yours. You can take her as your wife, and even if you don't love her, there are other ways to ensure you're happy."

I spin on my heel to face him. "Like you've done? Taking mistresses when mother is at home, waiting for you to return?" My words are filled with venom, dripping violently in the space between us.

"You're the Prince," he smirks. "You can do as you wish." He means that I'll be stepping into his shoes one day when I'm twenty-one. The asshole King of Chicago named so by his acquaintances who obey him daily.

"I want nothing of yours," I bite out. Frustration grips my gut, holding it fiercely, and I can't breathe. I'm never going to be like him. He'll have to kill me first.

"You know the legacy is there for you. You're in it by blood," he tells me. "You will be like me even if *you attempt to run away, Logan."*

"I'll never be a monster," I rage, turning on my heel and getting into the driver's seat of my car. I know he'll track my movements. He's done that all my life, but this time, I'll make sure it's the last time. I'm twenty fucking years old. I'm done being his lackey.

I speed down the drive and out through the metal gates that slide open, allowing me to leave. I'll be disowned if I don't obey him, but I'll make it easy for him. I don't need him or his blood money.

My grandfather's inheritance was bequeathed to me after he died, so I have a nest egg just waiting for me to claim it. And I'll finally do it because I need to get out from under my father's thumb.

My mind momentarily flits back to the girl. She's so young, and her life is already being mapped out for her. It makes me feel sorry for her, just for a moment, though. I shove the feeling away and focus on leaving the Oakridge house for good.

That was the last time I was on my father's radar. But I never stopped thinking about the girl I was meant to take as my wife. The same girl that now lives in a small town where she hides away from . . . something.

Was she given to another? Is that why she's in this shithole town?

Well, she doesn't need to hide anymore because she's mine. She was mine first and foremost, and I'm here to collect. I doubt she'll recognize me. She was only ten when she first saw me, and it was also the last time she laid her pretty eyes on me.

Back at the hotel, I open my laptop the moment I get into the room and log in. The browser loads and I type in my username and password. With a smile, I see two notifications waiting for me.

SB: I have to admit I'm scared. But I'm also confused at why you'd send me something instead of just introducing yourself. Are you some weird creeper? Like, I mean, are you going to stalk me now? I'm not sure I feel safe. I want to log off here and never return. But you already know where I am.

That's the end of message one, and I consider her fear for a moment. She should be fearful because it's dangerous to be talking to anyone online. *Doesn't she know that?*

SB: *Can we meet in the coffee shop on Main? I'd like to sit down and talk to you face-to-face. Would it be so wrong of us to perhaps see how this is going to go? You've found me, so let me know you.*

I consider this. Perhaps I can let her know me. Perhaps I can tell her I'm just a random person who is interested in her because we connected on a level that most women can't with me. But then I realize if she does recognize me, she'll know I sought her out. I tracked her since the moment she turned eighteen, and then when my contact found out she was on this shitty site, I signed up just to learn more about her.

I never made contact before. I waited, bided my time, and now that I'm here, I'm having second thoughts. It's not right what I'm doing, but then again, I grew up with a man who will do anything to make money, even if it's illegal. *What about my life is right?*

The carnal hunter who lives in my soul yearns for the chase. And I wonder if she'll

CHAPTER FOUR
Vera

IN MY APARTMENT, I OPEN MY LAPTOP AND FIND a response from him.

BP: Would you run when I come for you? I'm not a man who sits in a coffee shop to talk. I have violence in my blood and sin in my veins. And nothing you can do can change me.

Frowning, I think about what he means. He doesn't realize what I grew up with. My family is far from perfect. I grew up around violence and destruction, and the sins of my father and his acquaintances have made sure that my past is littered with overheard threats, with gunshots ringing in my ears, and most of all, the fear of being forced into a marriage of convenience that I ran away from.

I know if they find me, they'll push me down the aisle, make me say "I do," and then I'll be made to bear the children of the asshole my father has practically sold me to. But Dad is in prison, and he has no way of keeping me safe now. The man who was supposed to be my husband ran, he saw me and left, and my father brokered a new deal to have me married off to his father, the man I knew to be Dad's best friend. Older, unforgiving, and just as volatile as a criminal that needed to be locked up.

That wasn't happening, at least not under my watch. So, I ran away. At eighteen, I left the home I grew up in and found myself here, in Pine Lake. I managed to use my father's old contacts to buy a new identity. The moment I had the documents, I pulled a trigger to make sure he couldn't run his mouth off and cried for months. But I knew the moment I walked out, they would call the man I was meant to be bedding on my eighteenth birthday and inform him where I am.

One thing I learned from my father's

mistakes is that you should never leave a trail. My mind wanders to the man, to the *prince*, and I wonder if he knows who Herbert is. *Does he work for him? Is that why he found out where I lived?*

No.

If he did, I'd be dead already, or worse. I would be kidnapped and taken to the Oakridge house, where I know the man does terrible things to good people. He's evil, and if he found me, I'd be tortured for running. Herbert Oakridge isn't someone who just gives in, or forgives easily, and what I did will only earn me death by his hand.

SB: What if I didn't want to change you? I've lived my life with violent men, and I've grown up around sinful acts. I've watched things that no girl my age should. Danger doesn't scare me. It's the emotion that comes with allowing someone in that forces fear into my gut. Into my soul. Then we don't meet at a coffee shop. Perhaps we meet somewhere private. The park, at sunset. There's a small blue bench that overlooks the town. I'll be waiting.

I hit send. Then I move to the closet and pull

open the door. The box that's been gathering dust sits on the top shelf, half-hidden, but still visible for when I need it. I haven't touched the items inside for over a year. When I was seventeen, I watched my father get taken to prison. When Dad told me that I had to be careful, I knew something was wrong. Even though he signed the contract for me to marry Herbert, there was something else he didn't tell me. And now I can't even contact him to get the truth out of him.

I stood aside and saw how they cuffed his hands behind his back. There was nothing I could do but look on as the tears streamed down my face. And in that moment, I knew if I stayed, Herbert would make me his bride. Even though I was a teenager and he was an almost fifty-five-year-old man.

I lift the lid of the box and find the custom-made gun sitting in the holster. It was carved from metal and marble with my initials in the grip. My father gave it to me on the day of my seventeenth birthday. I hid it away until I needed it the day I collected my new identification. And now, the second time I'm holding it since *that* day I shot a man, I feel uneasy. I strap the holster around my thigh before slipping on black shorts that fall just below the weapon.

I have about thirty minutes before sunset, and I hope he sees the message before then. I'll wait for an hour. If he doesn't come, I walk away forever. And if he does, then I can try to find out if he's working for the old man. That's why I have the weapon. I may not have been trained to properly use it, but I know how to unlatch the safety, point, aim, and shoot. I've done it before, and I can do it again.

My computer speakers alert me of a new message causing my body to still and my stomach to flip-flop wildly. The bench I suggested we meet at has cameras overlooking it. He doesn't realize the town has a security system that is monitored, so even if something happens, it will be on video.

I open the message and find his words staring back at me.

BP: *The park it is. Till sunset, Beauty.*

❧

It's been almost an hour. I don't *feel* as if anyone is watching me. But I'm nervous all the same. I keep turning my head, looking left, right, and even behind me, but I don't see anyone making their way toward me. I should've brought my air pods. Perhaps music would've calmed me down somewhat, but then I wouldn't have heard if anyone was approaching.

The sun is almost gone, the sky a bright orange filtering off into dark red. It's always so beautiful at this time of day. Normally, I'd be running through the trees, maybe even all the way up to the lake. But for now, I'm sitting on the park bench, flicking through social media I no longer use.

The life I left behind halted the day before I ran off. The photos of my past staring back at me, reminding me of a time before all the bad shit went down, and for a moment, I miss it. My friends, the college I wanted to attend.

My dad was meant to keep me safe, not have me *sold off* to someone. Sadly, the marriage he had arranged wasn't something I wanted. He never asked my permission, and he never allowed me to speak up about my feelings.

All those memories are shadowed in darkness now. I blink, allowing a tear to fall, and then I quickly swipe it away. I don't need to get melancholy right now; I need to keep my focus on my surroundings.

I'm about to stand when a hand lands on my mouth, silencing a scream attempting to tear from my lungs. The hot breath of *him* is on my neck, and my heart leaps into my throat as fear grips me.

"Don't scream, Beauty," he murmurs. "I'm not going to hurt you, I just . . . I can't show you my face, and this was the only way to do this." He doesn't move his hand, but his lips whisper along my cheek. I could grab my gun; I could shoot it into the air and alert passersby that I'm afraid, but I don't.

I nod, hoping he'll release me.

"Once I move my hand, I need you to keep looking forward. You wanted to talk; I'm here to talk. But that's all I can offer you."

I nod again, my eyes shut tight as I pray silently that he's not going to pull a knife on me. But for some unknown reason, I feel confident that if I need to, I can run. We're in a fairly public place, and if I scream, someone will definitely hear me.

Slowly, his hand moves and my mouth is free. He trusts me not to scream. I can feel his heat, but he doesn't touch me. I don't turn around because I promised him I wouldn't, so instead of looking into his eyes, I look ahead of me.

"Why did you want to meet?" His voice is a deep baritone filled with gravel. There's also a hint of confusion in his words.

"Because you understood," I tell him.

Silence greets me, and I wonder if he walked away, silently, just like he appeared. But then he responds, "I do. I grew up around darkness, and I became it."

"I don't believe that."

"Why?"

"Because if you were, you would've hurt me already."

"Is that why you brought a gun?" he challenges, forcing a gasp of surprise to tumble from my mouth. "I can see the holster strapped to your thigh."

"I had to protect myself."

"It's stupid of you to come here." He's right; it was stupid, but I trusted my gut. Intuition has never led me astray.

"Perhaps." I lean back against the cool wooden bench. The feel of him closer now, and I wonder what he looks like. "Why don't you want me to see you?"

"Because if you do, I can't promise I'll be able to let you go." His words spike a shiver that races through me. There's a dark promise there, hiding in plain sight.

"Then you're just like the men I grew up around."

"Were they bad like me?"

I laugh. "Yes, more so. I was promised to a man when I was seventeen. He wasn't the first, though. He was my father's second choice."

"An arranged marriage?"

I nod.

"Tell me about the first choice. Why aren't you with him?" he asks, and I think back to that day. I was ten. My birthday party was in full swing, and my father pulled me aside to introduce me to two men. One old and gray, and the other, he was like a prince from my fairytale books. But he wasn't happy. He was so angry, and then he looked at me like I was annoying before he turned around and walked away. It was the first and last time I ever saw him.

"He didn't want me."

"Why?" the stranger asks, curiosity pinching the word, as if he's pained for asking me such a question. My heart aches when I recall not being wanted. It only really sank in years later that even before I could understand the way the heart worked, a man who could've saved me didn't want me at all.

"Because he thought I wasn't good enough." It's not the whole truth, and it's not a whole lie. I leave out the part that my father was selling me off at the age of ten. There's more silence, but this time I know he's still there because I hear him breathe.

"That can't be true," he tells me. "He would've been an idiot to not notice your beauty," he continues as if I weren't even here. As if he were trying to convince himself of this fact. "He lost out, and now you're here."

"With you," I tack on, wondering if he'll disagree, but he doesn't. "Why can't I see you?"

My body is alert, needing to know what this man looks like, but I don't turn. He asked me not to, so I obey, but my restraint is wearing thin.

"What is your name, Beauty?"

"You don't need me to tell you my name," I tell him. "Because you already have it, or you wouldn't have found me."

"Your IP address gave away your location, beautiful girl," he chuckles, and I picture him shaking his head at my naivety. "Tell me your name?"

"Tell me yours," I counter, and another laugh bounces through his chest, and I smile to myself as I shut my eyes. I decide I love the sound.

"You're a feisty one."

"Does it turn you on?" I question easily. This is like chatting to him online. I can't see his reaction, and it makes me braver than I should be.

Once again, I feel the heat of his breath on my neck, and a small whimper escapes me. The soft whispering of his lips tingles along my ear before he responds, "Do you want to turn me on? You did a good job of doing that last night."

I gasp, my eyes snapping open as I stare up at the sky, my head tipped to the side, giving him access to me. "What?"

"I was hard for you. Reading your words, I pictured you sleeping soundly in your bed as I made my way into your bedroom. I would tug at the sheet covering your lithe frame, and then I'd stare at how beautiful you look in those tight panties and your tank top. While I watched the rise and fall of your perfect tits, I'd stroke myself."

Every dark whispered word falls from his mouth and trickles its way from my ear down to my nipples, hardening them, and then traveling to my core. I squirm on the seat, the image he's painting vivid in my mind.

"I'd take my cock out, hard and needy, but I wouldn't touch you because just the thought of your porcelain skin under my fingertips brings out a beast within me. And then I'd grip my shaft and slowly move my hand up and down, making the tip of me glisten with arousal. The image of me painting your soft parted lips with my precum dances in my mind, and I lean in to do just that. My sweet Sleeping Beauty."

The moment his words halt, a cold shiver races down my spine, and I spin around, finding nobody there. Not a shadow, not even a noise of his shoes moving away. I'm on my feet in seconds, running down the hilltop, but I don't see anyone who could be the man who just gave me my ultimate fantasy with mere words. I'm alone, my panties are wet, and all I can think about is him doing all those things he promised me.

I stand there in the dark, wrapping my arms around my middle, and I wonder if he's watching me from the shadows. If he's there, hiding and waiting. *Would he steal me? Would he break into my bedroom and really do that?*

I make my way home with my head still filled with the images he painted with his deep voice. Every utterance causing goosebumps to rise in the wake of his pained promise. He obviously doesn't work for Mr. Oakridge. He couldn't, because if he did, he would've snatched me right there in the park. He would've hurt me. But what doesn't make sense is why he ran.

CHAPTER FIVE
Logan

SHE'S FUCKING WITH MY HEAD. I WAS SO CLOSE to showing her who I am. The same man who snubbed her years ago. But she's no longer the little girl I recall looking up at me like I was her savior. Now she's a grown woman looking for a prince. But I'm so far from royalty, my needs far more dangerous than she can even fathom.

I pick up my cell phone and turn it on. I needed to get away from her the moment I told her my fantasy of how I'd love to find pleasure with her body unmoving, her sleeping form merely a toy for my amusement.

I tap out a message to the one man I can still trust. He may have previously worked for my father, but I've known him since I was a kid. He was the one who helped me track my beauty, and now he's going to ensure that this arranged marriage farce is dealt with. I need to know who she's been promised to, and the moment I find out the name, I'll gut the asshole myself.

My phone rings five minutes after I hit send. I grin as his name comes up on the screen, and I answer immediately. "What's up, fucker?"

"You are contacting me, so that means something is bothering you, Logan," he speaks in the thick accent I've come to know well. We grew up together. We're both heading toward our thirties, and when we were younger, we promised the other that our friendship far outweighed the bullshit of our parents.

"I made contact with her. I spoke to her," I tell him urgently. I'm sure he can tell from the sound of my voice I'm concerned. "She said something to me that's got me thinking—"

"Is this about her engagement that her father had promised?"

"You knew about it? Who is it? I need to know because the moment you give me a name, I'll find the asshole, and I'll make sure he sings like a goddamned canary."

Dax sighs on the other end of the line. "I did know, but the problem is, you can't kill the man she's been promised to."

"What? Why?"

He's silent for a moment, and I wonder what the fuck he's hiding from me. The dickhead may be my friend, but he needs to tell me right the fuck now.

"She ran off just before her eighteenth birthday, and he's been searching for her ever since. If he finds her . . ." His warning is clear, even though he doesn't finish the sentence, I know Vera is in danger. Real danger, not the playful, roleplaying that she needs so badly. "The man in question, he's not someone you want to fuck with."

"Dax, I'm not fucking around any—"

"It's your father."

The breath whooshes out of me in one heavy swoop. He has to be fucking kidding me. *My father with Vera? What the fuck is he thinking?* Surely, my mother knows about it. She has to. Perhaps that's why she's been calling me nonstop.

My mind calculates the fallout from this. If my father wants her, he'll have to go through me. I may have walked away from her once, but I'm not doing that again. There is no love lost between my dad and me, and this would definitely kill any lingering doubt.

"What if I took her?"

"Then it will be your head he's searching for," Dax warns. "Listen to me, Logan, I may have done some stupid shit before, but this is taking on the king. You do realize that it could get you killed," he tells me.

This is not news to me. My father has the connections, he has a fucking army behind him, and me, all I have is her. But then again, once she learns who I am, she'll only hate me even more.

"I know. I . . . I need to do this."

"He's going to be at the club tonight. I can try to get some information out of him. He still trusts me even though Theia's dad was his friend." Dax can do this. Theia, Dax's submissive, grew up around the same men Vera did. Dangerous and violent. And her father was one of the worst. Thankfully, her brothers,

Samael and Kael, didn't turn out like their dad.

"He can't know where I am, Dax."

"I'm not going to throw you into the lion's den," he tells me. "And you know I have the Wolfes on our side." He's talking about Samael, Axel, and Kael. They'll step in if needed. I haven't seen them in years.

"Do it. Just leave her out of whatever the hell you're going to talk to him about. I don't want her name coming up. If it does, shut it down. Contact me once you have more."

"What will you do with the girl?" he asks, knowing I can't let her be captured by my father and his fucking squad of murderers.

I don't have to think twice about my answer, and it falls freely from my lips. "Take her and keep her." He knows what that means. Sometimes, to be the hero, you have to be the villain too. And nobody knows that better than the man I'm currently talking to.

"Fine. Don't show your face around until I contact you."

I nod before realizing he can't see me. "Sure, I'll wait."

I have to somehow get her alone again.

Once I can, I'll snatch her and keep her safe. Her life hangs in the balance. The sooner I can get her out of this town, the easier it will be to let Dax do his thing.

"Will you handle Herbert?"

"With pleasure." I hear the satisfaction in his voice. I'm not averse to getting my hands bloody, but my focus is on Vera. Having her safely stowed away will be best for her. But for me, it might just fucking kill me.

"Good luck," I tell him.

"I don't need luck, Logan." I nod even though I know he can't see me. I hang up before he has time to say anything more. I'm about to kidnap the woman who's trusted me so far. *Would that break her trust?* Or will she be able to see this for what it is—me saving her life?

I open my laptop, log into the browser, and find a message from her.

SB: *You ran. I wanted to see you. Those things you said, you didn't scare me. Perhaps you're right. I'm a stupid little girl who's about to get herself into trouble. But all I needed, ached for, was to see your face as you told me those desires. They're dark, but* *they're something I need to hear, that I want to hear. Is that something you promise? Or is it something you told me to make me ache for you even more? Tell me . . .*

She's slowly flaying me open, giving me the answers I crave so badly. The monster inside bares his teeth, and I can't stop the growl that vibrates through my chest. She's unnerving me. *How can someone so young, so innocent and naïve, crave such darkness?*

I sit back and decide how to respond. She already trusts me, but to steal her away from a life she's built for herself is another thing altogether. She believes I walked away all those years ago because I thought she wasn't good enough, but she couldn't be more wrong about that.

Besides the anger toward my father, it was the fact that I knew she'd grow up to be pure. And I would be the impurity that would only corrupt her. But now that I've made contact, I can't just leave her here to be taken by that old asshole. And there's about to be a war, where my beauty will be used against me.

I finally decide on my response. I need her to accept that her life will be with me, hidden in the shadows until Dax can finish this war we're about to wage on my father. He doesn't realize I'm still in contact with Dax, and thankfully, my friend isn't going to tell him.

I have time, but I need to make my move soon. They're not going to sit around and wait for me to decide between doing right and wrong. They're going to attack, and I need Vera to be safe by the time that happens.

So, with a sigh, I allow my fingers to offer her a response, as it bleeds directly from my heart.

BP: You shouldn't ache for a monster, Beauty. It's what will get you hurt, maybe even killed. My face is unimportant because the moment you see it, our fantasy is over. Isn't this meant to be just that—a fantasy? This is no longer a game to me. Your scent drove me wild with need; your sweetness and purity will be tarnished with my darkness and violence. I need you to tell me honestly . . . Is this something you want? Me? Because if it is, I'll make it so. The fear that turns you on will intensify. I'm not a gentle man. I'm not a soft and affectionate person. When I take you, and yes, that's a when not an if, it will be harsh and brutish. I will push your limits and test your boundaries. And when I'm done, you'll be mine. Tell me, yes, and I'll come for you.

After I hit send, I picture her sitting on her bed, reading my words. I even imagine her touching herself to the dark promises, because I know that's what she would do. I want to see what she looks like when her body finds release. I want to watch her shiver and tremble as she comes wildly, bucking her hips. And I want to be the one who does that to her.

My father will never lay his hands on her.

She was mine first, and she will be mine last.

CHAPTER SIX
Vera

I DON'T KNOW HOW MANY TIMES I'VE READ HIS words. Again, and again, yet my body still responds the same way—with desire. Even though he promises pain, I have a feeling it's more a warning of what he is capable of than what he will do to me.

I have a gut feeling about him. Something that hits deep in my soul, and I wonder if I know this man from somewhere else. He asked about my past, about the reason I believed my suitor didn't want me. He listened so silently; I wonder if he was cursing the man who walked away from me.

I never knew why he left. My father never spoke of him again, but I know his friendship with the boy's father was still strong after that day. I don't recall why my father never unfriended the man afterward, but I remember the boy, Logan Phillip Oakridge. When I was older and I knew more about him, learning that he was known as the prince in Chicago, and his father a king of the criminal world, I was shocked. My father wouldn't sell me off to someone like that, but when Herbert walked in, I realized my father would've given me to anyone just to keep them happy.

I sat in Dad's office while he signed the agreement that I would become an Oakridge. I was a pawn in a game I had no experience playing. They all saw me as a little girl—innocent and stupid—yet they didn't realize I'm as intelligent as they are. I knew how to do my homework—I would snoop into my father's documents, read up all I could, and I taught myself what the business my dad dealt in truly was.

He had friends in bad places. They weren't the average businessmen you saw walking into high rises in the city. They were the men who hid in the shadows until nightfall to take what wasn't theirs to take.

I pick up the mug I set down earlier, taking a sip of the now-cold coffee. I can't tear my gaze away from the computer screen, yet I'm zoning out, thinking back to all those times I found more and more information on what my father was doing.

When he got arrested, I wasn't angry because I knew he wasn't a good man. Anyone who works with Herbert isn't good. But this stranger, he's not like them. Then again, I don't know if I can trust my gut right now.

SB: I want that, but . . . It's only been two days. I wanted to see your face to know who you are. Is that so wrong since you know who I am? I've grown up around bad men, but when I was with you, near you, I didn't get the feeling you were all that bad. Why do you persist on warning me away from you? I may only be twenty, but I'm far from stupid. I had to grow up fast, and I have a feeling you know more about that than you're letting on. If you know so much about me already, you'll know I'm hiding. I'm running from my past. But then again, so are you. Aren't you?

I hit send, unsure what he's going to say to that, but I want the truth. If he can't give me that, then this ends right here. Confusion settles in my mind. I sip the coffee, wincing at the coolness of it, but I don't get up to heat it or grab a new mug. Instead, I sit and watch the screen until the ding sounds.

BP: I know more about running than most. And yes, I do know you're hiding. The question is—why would you trust me when you're running from a man? What if I'm working for him? What if I hurt you, physically? I want nothing more than to steal you away, Beauty. I'd like to take you to a place where no one will ever find you, but the moment I do that, you're putting your fragile life in my hands. Is that something you can live with?

He's right. He still could hurt me, kill me even. But that would happen the moment Herbert walks in here and takes me anyway. A man like that won't accept that a woman doesn't want him. He's ruthless, but I have a feeling this man, this stranger, is not the same. I can't explain what I feel for my Broken Prince.

I hit send before I get up and head to the kitchen. I've done stupid things before, but this is by far the most intense of them all. Since running away, I've been careful about who I contact, knowing anyone could be working for the Oakridges.

I wish I had someone to call. Someone I could trust. But there's no one in my life. My father made sure I was alone, and when I left, I walked out with nothing except the money Herbert didn't know about.

If my father ever did one good thing in his life, it would be that. The message I've been waiting for comes through at that moment, and I settle on the sofa, pick up my laptop, and set it on my crossed legs.

BP: I had a chance to do a lot, but I'm not that kind of man. When I take you, it will be because you want it. I'm worried that you're walking into this with your eyes closed because you think you know what bad men do. Maybe you do, but you have to take care of yourself. Think about the future rather than the need you have right now. If I were at your door right this minute, would you run, Beauty?

I ponder this. I'm very aware that this is dangerous, yet I can't shake the feeling of wanting to know this man. More so than I already do. But I don't respond just yet, I shut my laptop and curl up on the couch with my blanket and close my eyes. It's dark out, and today has been tiring. My eyes flutter, and a familiar shiver trickles its way down my back.

I startle awake, a noise drawing me out of dreams of a faceless stranger. I blink once, twice, and by the third time, I open my eyes to find I'm still on the couch. But the curtain is blowing in the early morning breeze, causing me to shiver.

The sun is just about peeking over the horizon, and the sky is a strange purple-orange blend of shades. Furrowing my brow, I push off the cushions and head to the window, shutting it with a loud thud.

My heart catapults when I see a shadow moving from the building, where the fire escape ladder squeaks, as the figure races down the road. I can't make out who it is, but I have a feeling it's someone I know. Perhaps not personally, but I know him better than he thinks.

I head into the kitchen once the window is latched and flick on the Keurig machine. Setting the mug under the drip, I look out the kitchen window and stare at the gray clouds fighting their way in front of the rising sun.

I think back to last night and the message from the stranger. I wonder what his name is. He hasn't told me that. And I figure I need to ask him again. When I brought it up before, he brushed it off, refusing to answer my question, yet he knows who I am.

In the living room, I grab my laptop and

set it on my desk before settling into my chair. Opening the lid, I turn it on and log in. I open my emails first, finding one from my lecturer asking about my assignment. I'm falling behind, and I blame my intrigue on the stranger. Once I've responded asking for an extension, I allow my Word app to open while I tap out the website address I've wanted to visit since I first logged in.

The moment my profile blinks on, a messenger window opens, and I see he's online. My heart thrums against my ribs, reminding me of why I'm awake so early. The noise, the window, and the shadowy figure racing from my apartment building.

BP: *Good morning, Beauty.*

I smile at the name that he's taken to calling me, but then a frown mars my happy face.

SB: *Were you at my window this morning?*

BP: *Cutting right to the chase? I like it. Yes, I was.*

Again, my heart attacks my ribs. Did he break into my apartment?

SB: Why? You woke me up with a noise. Did you mean to?

BP: I didn't. I like watching you sleep. Do you remember the first time I told you about my desires?

SB: Yes.

BP: Well, one of them is watching you sleep. I . . . I have an affliction. I'm not sure where it comes from, or why I feel it, but when I see a woman asleep, unconscious, it turns me on.

SB: So, you're stalking me and watching me sleep while you're . . . turned on?

BP: Long answer or short answer?

SB: Don't bullshit me. I need to know. I'm not going to turn you in, but I need to know everything about this situation. I know that this situation isn't normal, that's clear, but if I'm meant to trust you, surely you can give me something to trust.

BP: *I like you, feisty. And yes, I was hard looking at you. All I could think about was painting your pretty face with my seed. And I craved it. I told you, Beauty, I'm not a good man. Not at all. I'm broken, and my mind tends to lead me into dark corners when I wish I could be normal.*

What does that even mean? I stare at the screen for a long while, trying to figure out what he's talking about, but before I can respond, another message comes through from him.

BP: *Let me keep you safe. From everything.*

Safe. It's a relative word to me because nothing I can do will ever keep me safe forever. Eventually, they'll find me, and when they do, my life will no longer be my own. *What can another man, perhaps just as dangerous, offer me?* Nothing more than a bodyguard who would be taken down the moment Herbert and his men step into the ring with him.

SB: I can't ask you to do that. It's my life, and I need to live it out the way I choose.

BP: Meet me in the park. Just once more, and I'll try to show you that I'm worthy of your trust. Please.

The sun is high now, streaming through my living room windows, which overlook the meadow, and I take note of the bench where I sat only hours ago. It feels like a lifetime. I consider his offer, if he wants to meet, perhaps I can give him that much.

SB: Okay. Give me an hour.

BP: Why? You going to make yourself look pretty for me, Beauty?

I laugh out loud, but I also feel heat blooming in my cheeks. I'll get to see him. The thought of finally seeing his face makes my stomach tumble wildly.

SB: Perhaps. I'll see you soon.

I log off before I'm tempted to ask him any more questions. I head into the bathroom to freshen up before I make my way into my bedroom and find a pretty summer dress, along with a denim jacket, which I shrug on before pushing my feet into a pair of Doc Martens that have seen better days. I look like a crazy hippie with my mismatched colors, but I don't care. This is who I am now, someone so opposite of who I was that at times I don't recognize myself.

With fifteen minutes to spare, I make my way out of the apartment and onto the road, taking the path up toward the same bench from earlier. My phone is in my pocket if I need it, and I have a small pocketknife chained to my keys.

I've been wary for a long time, and even though I've come out here before, I've always kept my knife on me. It's tiny, but it will do some damage. I'm definitely not trained to fight, but I can hold my own.

I settle on the bench, taking in the people heading out for a morning run or breakfast at the local café, and even those walking their dogs.

This is fine; I'll be okay. I swallow the lump in my throat, forcing myself to calm down, but the flip-flop in my stomach doesn't ease.

I'm about to take a short walk toward the trees when someone slumps beside me on the bench. He's wearing a dark hoodie, along with a baseball cap, which hides part of his face.

"You came," I speak. My voice is scratchy, filled with both excitement and trepidation. *Why won't he show me his face?*

CHAPTER SEVEN
Logan

THOSE TWO WORDS ARE THE BALM TO MY EVER-aching heart. I made a mistake with her all those years ago, and I promise myself now that I won't do it again. When she agreed to meet me, I decided it's now or never. If I show her my face, she'll hate me.

I can do it right now, and while I wait for her to recognize me, I know I'll hold my breath, and it will be the end of my secrets. Can I let go of that part of me? The desire that coils itself around my veins, thrumming through my blood. If she does know who I am, I'll have to explain why I walked away from her.

Silently, I weigh my options, but I don't move. The hoodie covers my face, and I don't turn to her, yet being beside her makes me want to show her who I am. Need fires inside me, sparking the coldness into heat that sears every inch of my body.

I want nothing more than to look into her eyes and see her beautiful face without hiding. But for now, I sit and look ahead of me. I can feel her staring, waiting. I know the moment I look into her eyes for the first time in nine, almost ten years will be jarring.

When I first met her, she was pretty, cute, but now she's a woman, all grown up, and I need to be prepared for the effect she will no doubt have on me.

"I came," I tell her, but she's still staring. I inhale a deep breath before I finally decide to do it. I push back the hoodie of my jacket and glance her way. The breath I took whooshes from my lungs in one fell swoop. Her eyes are like gems as they pierce me right to the very fucking core.

If she recognizes me, she doesn't say anything about it. Silence stretches between us like a wire tugged taut, ready to snap. A smile tilts her pouty lips up. They're not shimmering, merely soft and wet from the way her tongue darts out, and she licks at them nervously.

"I didn't think I'd see your face," she says, but there's still no recognition in her eyes.

"And? Was it everything you thought it would be?" I ask, smirking as she blushes a deeper shade of pink. Her soft, porcelain skin reminds me of those collectible dolls you find at antique stores. Untouchable, beautiful, fragile. And that's what she is.

I must remind myself that no matter what her desires are, this girl is nothing short of breakable. I could so easily make her cry, make her scream, and that thought doesn't do all that much for me like the thought of her under me while she's asleep. And that's where my depraved mind goes as I look at her.

"Perhaps," she tells me. "I don't know why I'm doing this." Her voice breaks, but I watch her swallow down whatever emotion suddenly appears, and she shakes her head. "A long time ago, I thought someone would save me from myself, from my life. My father wasn't a good man — well, isn't — since he's still alive."

"You don't have to tell me anything you

don't want to."

She ignores me and continues, "He brought someone to me on my birthday, told me he was the man I would marry one day." My chest caves in, and I am certain she's about to confess that she knows who I am. Surely, she does.

"And then?"

"Like I told you before, he didn't want me."

"Why wouldn't he want you?" I lean my elbows on my thighs, looking at her over my shoulder. Those gorgeous, jewel-like eyes shimmer with emotion. If she blinks, her tears will fall, and I picture what she'll look like with makeup streaked across her face.

"I don't blame him. I was only ten at the time."

"What if he walked back into your life right now?" I don't know why I ask this. That's a lie; I do know. I want her to tell me she'll accept me, the man who walked out and made sure her chances of surviving were shot to hell. Her father fucking sold her off to my father, and all for what?

"I would probably ask him why he hated me *that* much he'd allow my life to be shoved into the path of another bad man."

"What if it wasn't his choice?"

"Wasn't it?" she questions, finally meeting my gaze. "You walked away and left me there, wondering what was wrong with me." She knows who I am. The anger that simmers in her pretty eyes sparks something inside me, want and need, and something else. The need to make it right. To help her.

"Let me fix this and take you away."

"Why? So your guilt can ease from what you forced me into?" She's on her feet, her arms crossed in front of her chest, and I know soon enough she's going to walk away from me. But I can't let that happen. If I do, when all hell breaks loose back home, she's going to be in the line of fire.

"Yes," I answer honestly. I can't lie to her. She deserves the truth, and that's what she'll get from me. But I need to make her see the danger she's in. "If you don't want to come with me, I'll have to force you. There's a war coming, Beauty, and it's not going to be pretty. There will be casualties, and I don't want you to be one of them."

She stares at me for a long while. There's intrigue in her gaze and a million questions that flit across her expression. I want to answer them all, to give her the truths she didn't get for so long. But right now, my focus must be on getting her out of town.

The cabin.

It's safe, secluded, and it's the only place I know they won't look for her.

"Don't come back here," she tells me. "I thought you were someone else, someone who—"

"I need you to listen to me," I bite out, pushing to my feet, gripping her shoulders tightly. I want to pull her close to me, to hold her, but she shoves me away.

"No. I won't listen to you, or my father, or anyone else for that matter. I chose to hide from my life, and I'm not going to let you pull me back into that sordid mess."

"I'm trying to keep you safe."

"By lying to me?"

"Lying?" My brows furrow at her words. *How did I lie to her?*

"Broken Prince?" she scoffs. "Please, spare

me the pain and agony of your perfect life with all that money, status, and the fact that when you saw me, you sneered at me as if I were shit under your shoe."

"You were a fucking child!" Somehow, my outburst hits her hard, and she stumbles backward away from me. "You were a child," I say once more, this time less angry.

She nods. "I was. But we both grew up knowing our lives would be mapped out before us. And because of you, I have to live like this." She waves her hand around her at the town where she's been hiding.

"Things are happening that will put you in danger."

"More so now than I've been before?" she challenges. One thing I'm learning about sweet Vera Rose is that she's not the shy girl I thought she'd be.

"Yes." The one word hangs between us ominously, and I hope she can see the truth in my eyes because I can't tell her more than that until I've heard from Dax. Her father is in prison, so he won't be pulled into this shitshow, but she's here, bait for the sharks to find. And

CHAPTER EIGHT
Logan

IN THE HOTEL, I TRY ONCE MORE TO MAKE HER see the truth. If she doesn't want to listen to me face to face, I'm going to tell her word for word.

BP: *I'm not here to play games, Beauty. I may not be the first person you wanted in your life right now, but I'm here, and I won't allow you to get yourself hurt because of the past. Like I said, a war is coming, and you'll be a casualty if you don't trust me. One chance, that's all I need. Please.*

I hit send before I have time to second-guess myself. I'm frustrated, yet I can't stop thinking about how beautiful she looked when fire danced in her eyes. I head into the kitchen and find a beer. It's fucking ten in the morning, yet I'm swallowing back the alcohol like it's ten in the evening.

The computer dings, but I don't go to it. Instead, I head into the bedroom and pull out the suitcase I brought here a couple of days ago. Inside, I find what I need — the cloth, blindfold, cuffs, and the bottle filled with a drug that will ensure my sweet girl is asleep long enough for me to get her out of her apartment, into the car, and back to my cabin.

I wasn't lying to Vera when I told her I'd steal her away. Once all the items are laid out on the bed, I pack my clothes into the suitcase and set it at the door. Ready for me to leave at a moment's notice.

Once I know everything is cleaned, wiped down, and back to where it was before I entered the room, I pick up my laptop and find a response from Vera waiting for me.

SB: You chose to walk away. Don't try to lay your guilt on me by telling me you're here to play the hero. I don't need one, and I don't want one. I'll be

My chest tightens at her words. Even just the thought of never laying my eyes on her again takes the breath from my lungs. That can't happen, ever.

The night is clear, the moon slowly waning in the darkness, and the stars bright, shimmering prickles of diamonds in the ink of the sky. I'm dressed, the car is ready, and I have everything I need. I've never done this before, stolen someone from their home.

In the past, I wouldn't second-guess myself, but after learning about my father's dirty dealings, I feel like I'm turning into him. Even though I'm trying to save her, Vera isn't going to like the fact that I'm taking her without her permission.

Kidnapping.

Stalking.

All of this is wrong, but I can't stop myself now. As I drive down the main road and toward her building, I play out in my mind all the ways this could go wrong. She could scream. Her neighbors could call the cops. She could try to run, hurt herself.

Or it could be as simple as walking in, injecting her with the drug, and sweeping her into my arms and walking out of her apartment without anybody noticing.

I watch her window from the street, and I wonder if she can sense me here in the darkness. But she shuts her curtain before turning out the light. I wait, inhaling a deep breath, focusing on the job at hand.

When my father sent me out on jobs, I would be confident, didn't give a shit what happened to me, but this time, it's not only my life on the line. Perhaps that makes it even more dangerous than it should be.

I head down to the car and start the engine. I planned this over the past few days, and me slipping through her window was a test to see if I could do it. So, I know my way up and the way down. I pull onto a small back road and stop right behind her apartment block.

Thankfully, it's dark, and there doesn't seem

to be anybody lurking around. The rope and tape, along with the syringe, are all in hand as I ascend the steps. Nervousness sparks through me, and I silently ask for her forgiveness.

When I reach the second floor, I stop, listening for any noise from Vera's neighbor, but it seems the apartment is dead-quiet. Pulling my lockpicking device from my pocket, I crouch and work the door until I hear the familiar click.

It's so quiet I can hear my heart beating. The exhilaration of doing something *wrong* still sparks excitement in my veins. Inside the apartment, I make my way through the darkness, my eyes slowly adjusting to the surroundings as I move.

There's a lamp shining from inside her living room, which casts the rest of the apartment in a yellow shadow. When I reach her bedroom door, it's open, and there, on the king-sized bed, is my beauty.

She's asleep, her eyes closed, her body draped in the sheet, and her chest rising and falling gently as she dreams. I wonder briefly if I'm in those dreams. Am I on her mind as she lies unconscious?

My cock hardens painfully against my zipper when I move closer. Her nipples are hard against the smooth white material of her tank top. I pull the syringe from my pocket and tug the cap off before testing a small squirt of sedative.

When I lean in, I catch her scent, vanilla, and pine. It's an interesting combination, heady and sweet, yet so familiar I'm painfully aching to be with her, inside her.

The moment the needle enters her smooth, soft flesh, her eyes snap open, and her mouth gapes. But I'm faster, and my hand lands on her mouth, catching her scream in my palm. Her eyes are wide, fear shining in them as she tries to make out what is happening.

When she realizes it's me, she halts all fight, but I put that down to the drug rather than her accepting it's me about to steal her. Once her lashes flutter and she's asleep once more, I scoop her up and take her through to the living room where I lay her on the sofa.

I move quickly, grabbing a rucksack from her closet and filling it with clothes, her laptop, and some personal items from her nightstand, including the bracelet I gave her. She may not forgive me right away, but one day, she'll realize this is for her own good.

Once we're in the car, it doesn't take long for me to head out onto the highway and out of the small town she called home. The cabin is waiting, and I know soon enough, I'll have to keep her locked up until she comes to terms with her new home.

I can only pray it's enough to keep her safe.

CHAPTER NINE

Vera

A LOUD CRASH HAS ME SHOOTING UP FROM the soft mattress I'm lying on, and my eyes snap open in shock. My head feels groggy, and my throat is dry as if I had a whole bottle of wine last night.

The room I'm in is not mine. Nothing looks familiar, and I try to figure out where the hell I am. I take in the furniture, which is all oak, not the dark wood from my childhood home or the Ikea furniture from my apartment.

The walls are made of light wooden logs, thick and sturdy, and the small window to the left of the bed I'm on is shut tight. But from where I am, I can tell the view is no longer the small town I've come to love. All I see are trees.

The forest thick and lush, and the gray sky looming ominously overhead.

Another crash sounds from somewhere, and then last night flashes in my mind. The man, the stranger who is no longer a stranger. It's Logan. I remembered him the moment he showed me his face. Anger surges through me when I recall his words to me— *"The moment you turn your back on me, I'll follow you, and I will most certainly steal you from your life here."*

The asshole really fucking kidnapped me. Shooting to my feet, I head to the door, twisting the handle, but it's locked. I slam my palms against the wood, screaming at him to let me out.

"You asshole! I'm not fucking kidding, let me out!" My voice is hoarse, the words scratching against my throat. "Logan fucking Oakridge!" Again, he ignores me, or he can't hear me because I'm still alone a minute later.

I glance around the room, looking for something I can use as a weapon, but with every drawer I open, I come up empty. He wasn't kidding, and now I'm stuck in the middle of nowhere with that asshole.

I can't believe he came for me. When I was ten, I looked up at him, hoping he'd smile at me. Now all I want him to do is walk away from me like he did all those years ago. Guilt is a heavy burden to carry. But no matter what he does, he can't fix what he did.

Leaning against the wall beside the window, I slide down until my ass hits the floor. The coolness of the room makes me shiver. I don't know how long I sit there staring off into space when I hear footsteps outside the door. I want to move, to run toward it, but I don't feel like fighting him right now. Even if I tried, he's taller, bigger, and stronger than I am.

"Good morning, Beauty." He smiles, and even though it looks like a genuine grin, anger flares inside me, and I'm on my feet in seconds.

"What the fucking hell is wrong with you?" I shove against his chest, my fists no match for his hard muscles. The man is strong, wide, and tall. I have to tilt my head back to look at him. He's wearing glasses, the dark rims circling his almost-black eyes. Logan is no longer the young boy who sneered at me. He's a man, one who's looking at me as if he's about to devour me whole.

The flannel shirt he's wearing is unbuttoned, and I can't tear my gaze away from his smooth, inked chest underneath. The man is mammoth. I didn't notice it much when we were at the park, but now that we're both on similar ground, I can't stop staring. His dark hair is messily styled, sticking out in every direction. His angular jaw and sharp features look like they've been crafted with the finest materials by an artist who loved his work.

"I told you, Beauty," he speaks, dragging my attention back to the present and to the fact that he kidnapped me. "I won't let you get hurt."

"What you did was illegal!"

"It was. But then again, I'm an Oakridge. We've been doing illegal things since my grandfather took over from his dad and made friends with the gangs of Chicago." He shrugs as if this is normal, as if crime should be something to chat about over breakfast. At that thought, my stomach grumbles loudly, and Logan glances over me, his eyes trailing from my stomach up to my breasts then to my eyes.

"I can't be locked in here all the time." I

don't know why I'm saying that. It sounds like I'm accepting that this is normal, but the only thing I can think of right now is washing up and trying to find a way to make him let me go.

"Perhaps. But until you stop yelling at me to let you go, you'll spend your time in here." He doesn't look like he's joking. "When you learn that this will be your new home for the foreseeable future, then and only then will you be allowed freedoms like going into the garden."

"This is fucking ridiculous!"

He arches a brow at my outburst, and I force myself to rein it in. I'm more frustrated and angrier than I've ever been.

"You do realize that all this bullshit isn't going to work with me. Right?"

He doesn't respond, but he takes steps toward me, closing the distance, and he dwarfs my tiny frame until I'm backed against the wall. His eyes glower down at me, and I have to tilt my head backward to meet that dark gaze.

"I don't deal in bullshit. You're here because it's the only way to keep you safe. I don't give a shit if you hate me, if you want to hit me, or if you scream at me, I'm not letting you go."

"Safe from what?" I demand, hoping he has some way to explain himself. I know Herbert is out there, but since he hasn't mentioned that asshole, I think it is something else.

"Nothing you should concern yourself with."

"No. You're not allowed to just tell me shit like that and walk away. What are you keeping me safe from? Because if you can't tell me, then I know you're lying."

He sighs, and I wonder if he's annoyed with me. Perhaps he's second-guessing his choice to kidnap me and keep me in the middle of nowhere.

"Where are we anyway?"

"We're safe," he tells me. "Do you remember anything about the contract your father signed?"

His question stills me. Surely, he's not working for his father. If he was, he would've taken me there already. Logan watches me, waiting for a response. His eyes are piercing as he regards me. *Do I tell him what I know? Or is he trying to steal information to use against me later?*

"If you don't tell me, I'll find out for myself. I have friends in high places, Beauty," he offers, settling on the mattress, causing me to turn around and face him.

"Tell me about this war first," I respond, needing more information before I offer him everything I know about the man who wants me dead.

"My father is one of the most dangerous men in Chicago," Logan starts, and I nod because I know this already. I grew up hearing rumors about the king of the crime world. "He's wanted by people who would like nothing more than to see him falter. And I'm one of them."

"But don't you work for him?"

Logan shakes his head. "Not anymore, I didn't want that life. And no, I'm not the best person to be keeping you safe since my father's has connections, but I'm not letting him put his hands on you. It's . . ." His voice trails off, leaving silence in its wake.

"It's...?" I urge. "Logan, if you're not going to tell me, then you have to let me leave. I can't stay here. I have a life."

"You don't have a life out there. You're hiding out from Herbert. Being here, you'll be out of his line of fire."

"How do you know?" I cross my arms in front of my chest. "Let me go. Please?"

"No." He's on his feet, anger surging through him. He saunters to the door, twisting the handle and tugging it open. Soon enough, he's on the other side of the entrance. "Why can't you let me make this right?"

Frustration ebbs through me, flowing like a gushing river, and I can't stop the words from falling from my mouth. "Because you can't!"

He doesn't say a word. Just watches me for a long moment before he nods slowly, then shuts the door. I race toward it, slamming my palms against the wood, but I know he won't open it again.

I'm tired, hungry, and I feel hungover. I would love a bath or shower, just something that will calm me down, but I'm left alone in the room, and I don't know how long he's going to be gone this time.

I hear a car door slam, which has me racing for the window. I watch as Logan pulls away from the cabin in a blacked-out Range Rover. "Fuck!" My voice is hoarse, my throat burning as I stare at the dust the wheels kick up as he makes his way down the dirt road between the trees.

I'm alone, and I have no way of getting out of here.

CHAPTER TEN

Logan

Shaking my head, I pull up to the general store and get out of the vehicle. I'm still shaking, ready to put her over my lap and spank her pert little ass. But that's only going to make matters worse. I need to know more about her time with my father, but she doesn't trust me, not yet.

When I enter the store, the cashier looks up and smiles. She's been here every day since I moved up to the cabin. Thankfully, with the town being so small, it's quiet, and I can get feminine products, along with some soda, bread, and even some candy for Vera.

I didn't prepare to have her cooped up in my cabin for the unforeseeable future, but since she's acting like a brat, I'm going to have to ensure she has everything she needs. Once I've paid, I'm back in the truck in minutes.

The sun is still high, and I make a quick pitstop at the local bakery, where they have the freshest cakes and cookies. I buy a box filled with a variety of flavors before I head home.

The moment I pull up to the cabin, I look up and find Vera at the window, looking down at me. The bedroom has nothing that can aid her escape, but I can't deny I was worried she would be gone when I returned.

Inside, I set everything on the counter and listen to her screaming up a storm from the second floor as she tells me I'm a bad asshole, and she's going to kill me. I smile. The thought of her hurting me is laughable, but still, I can't help but wish we could have that fight while naked with her writhing beneath me.

I've never been able to find pleasure unless the woman is still asleep, not moving a muscle. The thought of controlling her body, while she is merely a rag doll for me to toy with, has always been my go-to. Sadly, not many women trust a man like that, not that I blame them.

The screaming upstairs stops, and I still for a moment. I want to go up there to see if she's okay, but I know I should let her blow off steam. Soon enough, she'll get hungry. She'll need to freshen up, and then she'll calm down. I pack the food in the cabinets before heading up with the toiletries I bought for Vera.

Once I've put them away, I move quietly toward her bedroom door and listen. It's silent, and I wonder if she's passed out. I wait another moment before I head downstairs to grab my phone. There's no news from Dax yet, but I know the moment he can, he'll make contact.

I pull out my laptop and log into the software I've used since I was fifteen. The program was coded by one of my father's men—an IT genius—which allows me to track Dad's whereabouts without his knowledge.

We used to use it for our clients, but now I use it to make sure I'm safe, and he hasn't found me. If I can get into the system, I'll try to find a link to Dad's contacts I know are trying to locate Vera. She's been lucky he hasn't found her yet.

I must try to get information about what he's up to because I have a feeling he's closing in on Vera; well, her old place. I log into the security systems at the apartment building she was staying in. I installed two small cameras before taking her, and I know they'll come in handy.

When I finally manage to get logged in, I find the place untouched. Flicking through both cameras, I make sure to note anything out of place, but I don't see anything. I'll give it another two days before checking again.

My email pings with an alert. I open it, flick through to the new message, and notice it's from an encrypted address. It must be Dax. I click it and scan the contents.

Logan,

He's making his play for her. He has his team searching, but I have a feeling he wasn't completely honest with me. There's something he's hiding, and I have my men on it. I can't promise you I'll have something before the weekend, but I'll try.

If you've already made your move, stay out of towns and cities. He is scouring the West Coast. He'll then head south, then east and north. I'm not sure where you are, but it's best that you don't come out of hiding until I've made sure the city is secure.

This isn't some idle threat. He's on the warpath. If he finds her, he isn't going to think twice about killing her. She ran, breaking a contract between him and her father. Which brings me to my next warning—her father is going to pay for this.

If you can keep that from her for the time being, it may make it easier for you to gain her trust. I'll see what I can do from my side, but all I can say is, be ready.

D.

I figured that's how it would go down. If Dax can get my father out of the way, perhaps I can go home. He didn't mention anything about my mother, but she's innocent in all this.

The floor creaks upstairs, and I decide to go back up to see if Vera is less fiery. Hopefully, she'll allow me to help her. Perhaps she can understand why I'm doing this. I take the steps two at a time, and I'm at her door in seconds. I unlock it before pushing it open to find her sitting on the bed. She's got her legs crossed, and I can't stop my gaze from wandering between her thighs.

Fuck.

I lift my gaze to meet hers. The corner of my mouth quirks as I regard her glare. "Are you ready to listen?" I ask her, but I don't make a move to enter the room. Instead, I lean against the doorframe and cross my arms in front of my chest.

"Are you ready to take me home?"

"No."

"Then no, I'm not ready to listen to your made-up stories," she pouts, and it's the cutest thing I've ever seen. How I walked away from her is beyond me. She turned into a beautiful young woman. I watch her squirm, and I can guess what she's struggling with.

"Do you need the bathroom?" I ask, gesturing with my chin toward her.

I can tell she's at war with herself. She wants to say yes, but she also wants to refuse my help. But this will only hurt her, not me. I shrug and take a step back before she shouts out.

"Wait!"

I do, stopping short, waiting for her to talk.

"Yes, please," she tells me. Her submissiveness makes my blood heat. It's been so long since I've spent so much time around a woman I can't help but notice the smallest quirks about her.

"And you're going to behave?" I challenge, knowing I'm going to piss her off. She may need me for certain things, but she's also got a stubborn streak that could put her at a disadvantage. I don't deal well with pouty little girls, and at the moment, she fits perfectly into that category.

I want her fire.

I want her to burn me from the inside out.

"I'll try," she bites out, pushing off the bed, her bare feet padding toward me. I grip her arm, tugging her along beside me. "I can walk on my own."

"Yeah? Then you'll be able to go to the toilet while I stand right here," I tell her as I lead her into the smaller room and wait at the door.

"No way," she grits through clenched teeth. Frustration etched on her pretty face, which only makes me smile. "I need privacy."

"You don't need shit. If you can't listen to me, or obey me, then you'll be under my surveillance twenty-four seven."

CHAPTER ELEVEN
Vera

*H*E'S SUCH AN ASSHOLE. I tug at my shorts and panties and sit down quickly, so he doesn't get a view of my ass. Embarrassment burns my cheeks, and the heat trails down to my chest. I must be bright red as I use the toilet while Logan stands only feet away. I've never been so degraded before, and it makes my stomach twist painfully.

Tears burn the back of my eyes, and I fight them back. I want to ask him why he's being such a dickhead, but I don't. Instead, I finish up, washing my hands and face and retying my ponytail.

"I'm done."

He nods, but I can tell he's still thinking

about what I asked earlier. He deflected the question, instead attempting to distract me from what I asked, but I didn't forget. His expression is reflective as he grips my arm once more and moves me toward the bedroom.

Once I'm inside, he leans against the doorframe again before asking, "What do you want to eat? I got some bread at the store so I can make a sandwich for you."

I watch him for a moment, wondering if this is my future, being held captive and fed like a child. I've been independent for a while now. I haven't had anyone look after me like this since I ran away from home, so this is difficult to accept.

"That will be nice, thank you. And . . . could I have some coffee or something, please?" I ask, my voice cracking at the thought of my freedom and dignity being stripped away in the blink of an eye.

"Sure." He tugs on the door, but I stop him with my hand on his arm before he can shut it. "What?" The word is strained, and I wonder if I'm truly annoying him, or if he's fighting the attraction. We did connect when we didn't know who the other person was. I know we did.

"Could I . . .? I mean . . ."

"Out with it, Vera," he sighs as if I'm frustrating him with my nervousness. *How does he expect me to behave? Does he want me to just love him because he apparently saved my life?* That's not how this is going to work, and he has to get it through his brain.

"Could I come down with you, please?" I attempt to give him my most submissive stare, praying he'll see I'm trying here.

"No." He tugs the door shut, and I hear the key turning and the lock falling into place once more. Sighing, I move toward the bed and settle on the mattress. Curling up, I stare out the window, taking in the gray clouds. The sun is trying to peek through, but it's hidden now. Earlier, it was warm in the room with the sunlight, but now that it's gone, a cold shiver trickles its way over me.

I shove the blankets down before slipping under them and pulling them up to my chin. My eyes feel heavy, but my stomach grumbles at the idea of getting a sandwich and some coffee.

My eyes open, and a scream lodges itself in my throat. Logan is standing over me, watching me with heated desire burning in his gaze. His hand planted firmly on his crotch, stroking himself gently through the material.

"What the hell are you doing?"

"I told you, Beauty, I love watching you sleep." The dark smile on his lips makes him look handsome, alluring, and dangerous at the same time.

Shock lances through me, and I realize he did tell me. He was honest. While we spoke online, he didn't hold back once he told me his needs.

"But," I mumble, unsure what to say. How can someone want that? I mean. It makes no sense to be turned on by . . . Shaking my head, I push up against the headboard. "I don't understand. Is that why you brought me here?"

"I brought you here to keep you safe."

"Yet, you're violating that safety." My words are harsh. Logan visibly winces at my retort, but before I have time to feel guilty for what I said, I tell him, "I mean . . . You can't just come in here and . . ." I wave my hand in the air, unsure how

116

to even describe what he was doing.

"I know. I mean, I brought your breakfast, and then I saw you lying there, beautiful, dreaming, and I couldn't stop myself." His words are pained. I don't have time to say anything more because he rushes from the room, slamming the door shut behind him.

Silence greets me. The room is suddenly colder, harsher than I remember it being before I fell asleep. I look up at the vanity and notice the tray sitting there. A steaming mug along with a plated sandwich call to me, and for a moment, I forget about our interaction because my stomach growls painfully.

I scoot to my feet, padding over to the vanity, and grab a piece of the sandwich, which he cut into small triangles, and I bite into the soft bread. It's still warm as if he'd just baked it himself, and the flavors of butter and cheese melt on my tongue. I can't help but groan in pleasure as the food finally makes its way down to my stomach.

I haven't eaten in a while, and this is delicious. I quickly finish the rest of the sandwich before I grab the coffee and settle back in bed.

The mug sits on the nightstand, and I glance out the window, noticing how the sky is slowly turning dark.

I've lost track of time being here. I can't imagine it's been more than a day, maybe two. But I have slept more than I have done in a long while. The door slides open after I hear the lock clicking, and Logan saunters in.

He makes his way toward me silently, setting down a stack of books before he turns for the door. He looks tense, his shoulders bunched, and his head bowed. Suddenly, I see the broken prince he claims to be.

"Wait."

He responds, "I'm not letting you out of this room, Vera," he mumbles under his breath.

"No, I . . ." My voice falters. I want to tell him something to keep him here. I feel lonely, and his presence, even though I'm still angry, makes it more bearable.

"Then what?" He glances at me over his shoulder. I notice the glasses he was wearing yesterday, rim dark eyes that look right through me. There's something haunted about him. A darkness I can't read, but it's there, creasing the corners of his eyes.

I have to admit he's handsome. He's tall, broad, and more man than boy. His angular jaw and sharp features make him look scary like he's a mountain man who could so easily fling me over his shoulder and saunter into the woods without anyone stopping him.

"Vera?" My name pulls me from the thoughts racing through my head.

"Can you sit with me?" Even though the question is whispered, I know he heard because his expression changes from angry to sad. "Just for a little while."

I don't know why I want him here, close by. But I do. There's a pull between us, something I can't deny because I feel it every time he's near me. As if we're magnets, a positive and negative being drawn together.

I don't know what to make of it.

But I know it's something dangerous.

CHAPTER TWELVE

Logan

WHAT CAN I SAY TO HER? How can I deny her?

I don't respond, but I do nod. I suppose it's my kind of reply. I turn and head for the chair, perched in the corner of her room. She eyes the door but then seems to think better of it. She should know that even if she makes it downstairs, there's no way she's getting out of the house. I've locked her in. Safely.

"Do you like living out here?" she asks, startling me because I didn't expect her to want to talk. I'm not sure I'm ready to speak about my life or what I need or want. Even though I gave her more of me through a website, I don't think she needs to hear about me face to face.

The anonymity of being online was easy. This? This is something completely different. It's dangerous. I can't let her get under my skin. And even as I think it, I know it's a lie because she's already there, burrowing her sweetness and innocence down into the depths of me.

She watches me, waiting for an answer, but I just shrug, pulling my phone out of my pocket and focusing on the email from Dax. Nothing more came after his initial email, and I know we'd be in more trouble if it weren't for him helping me.

I'm not sure how long it's going to take for them to get information, but I have a feeling my father will find her apartment before that happens.

"How long were you hiding out?" I ask her, but I don't look at her. I don't want to see the pain etched on her from knowing my father would marry her, bed her, and make her give him more children.

He may have waited until she was eighteen, but that doesn't excuse him from what he wants to do. I look up to see her staring out the window. She doesn't want to tell me, but I need to know.

"Vera, when did you run?"

"When I turned eighteen. I got one of my father's trusted contacts to make me new paperwork, ID card, passport, but I couldn't leave. I wanted to fly away, perhaps find a life in a new country, but I never got as far. The thought of leaving my father, even after what he did, wasn't something I wanted to do."

"So you stayed in harm's way?" I know I sound rude and callous, but the thought of my father finding her, touching her, has jealousy coursing through me. I want to kill the fucker for even attempting to marry her.

"And you're here because?" She turns to me. "If you hadn't walked out, I wouldn't have to live in captivity." Her anger is back, and it's warranted because she's right. But how could she even think I could want her back then? "All I wanted was a normal life," she tells me wistfully, but her eyes are trained on the window. On the forest beyond. Even if she did get out of the cabin, she wouldn't get far because there's nothing out there.

"And what exactly is a normal life?" I ask, wanting to give her that more than anything, but even though I do, I know it's impossible.

"A home somewhere scenic, a playful dog, maybe even someone who loves me. A partner who can take the darkness that courses through my veins and make me see it's not stupid or crazy. Someone who accepts that I need *those* things. Pleasure. Happiness. Things that normal people have."

"What about children?" I don't know why I ask, but it's something I need to know. For me. For her. I want nothing more than to take her, give her those things. I can head into town and find a dog for her. I can even take those dark desires and make them mine. She once accepted my needs, but then again, at the time, it was all fantasy. She wasn't really here. I wasn't really stalking her while she sleeps and getting myself off.

"Perhaps." There's a sad smile on her face, then she turns to me, directing those gem-like eyes on me, and I feel my heart kick against my ribs. The pain of the rhythm steals the breath from my lungs. "What about you?"

I'm not ready to talk about that. I wanted to know her, not spill my secrets to her right here and now. I shake my head, glancing away because I can't bring myself to admit what I want. I brought her here in the hopes that she'll be able to accept me in real life, not just online, but something tells me that's not going to happen.

"You can't want to know parts of me and not give me parts of you," she speaks, drawing my attention back to her. She's right. I know that. But I can't do this now. Pushing off the chair, I head for the door. I need to get out of this room that smells like her. Like promises and vows, I can never offer her.

I thought I could do this. I figured I could be the man who can offer her a forever, but I know I can't. She needs the prince, not a broken one, but someone who's good, who has light in his life. Mine is drenched in darkness.

Before I close the door, she calls out to me. "You can't hide forever, Logan." Her words pierce me right in the chest, lancing my heart, searing my veins. But I don't respond. Instead, I just close the door, locking it before I make my way downstairs.

When I reach the kitchen, I grab a mug and

fill it with black coffee, then I make my way outside. Settling on the bench, I sip the hot liquid while staring out at the trees. There's not much close by, and the silence is welcome. I hear banging from upstairs, and I know it's Vera once again trying to get my attention, but I need to be away from her for a while.

It's been a long time since I've been around anyone for this amount of time, and having her so close, knowing she's right there, is messing with my head. I'm so used to solitude that her voice breaks through the silence, reminding me of all I've done wrong.

Perhaps that's why I came up here. Hiding away from the guilt that seemed to follow me all those years ago. I didn't think it would bother me as much as it is. When I told Dax I'd take Vera, I thought it would be easy. Keep her here for a few weeks until my father is taken in, and then send her back home to Pine Lake.

But the more time I got to know her online, the more I read her messages, I know I can never let her go. She's too young for me, too innocent. I doubt she's even experienced half the things she fantasizes about; whereas, I've done far worse.

I sit back and think about her words once more. Pulling out my cell phone, I log into the website and pull up her profile. It's still there, taunting me. I open the inbox and slowly read through each and every response she offered.

Her words soothe, but they also burn. They remind me that I'm so fucking broken, and I close my eyes for a moment, willing my body to stop reacting to her. I've never had a woman who could satisfy me. I can't even fathom why, or what happened to me to make me so . . . depraved.

Perhaps I'm cursed. A prince cursed by a witch to forever live in darkness. And my princess is locked in a room where I can have her any time I want. But I would never force myself on her; she would need to ask me for it. And I know I'll gladly offer it up. I could make her ultimate fantasies a reality, and I think that's what scares her the most.

Because I know it scares the shit out of me too.

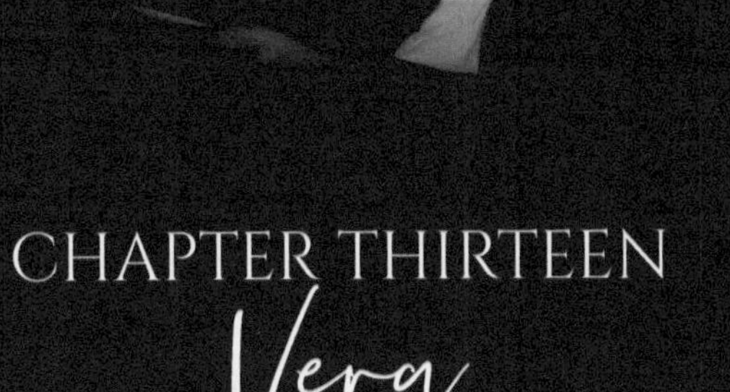

CHAPTER THIRTEEN
Vera

I'M LOST IN THE BOOK LOGAN LEFT EARLIER WHEN the door slides open, and he walks in with another tray. It's late. The sky is completely black, and I can't see much out the window.

"I've made something for dinner." He doesn't look at me as he sets it down, but he doesn't leave after he's done it either. Silence fills the space between us, which only frustrates me. I want him to talk to me. I need something. Living in this quiet is getting to me.

Pushing off the bed, I make my way toward him, stopping when I'm inches from him. The warmth of his body radiates through me, and my skin prickles with awareness. I think back to the moment I opened my eyes and saw him watching over me. His hand against the material of his crotch.

"Did you like it?" I mumble, looking up at him.

He avoids my gaze, but asks, "What?"

I take another step closer, which earns me a deep growl from the man who's now shut his eyes. Glasses still frame his perfect lashes as they flutter against his cheeks. Dark, just like his hair, they're fighting to stay down, and I ache to feel his gaze on me.

"Did you like seeing me asleep? Not moving, open for you. A lifeless doll for you to use as you please." I'm poking the bear, arousing him to the point of his hands fisting at his sides. But he doesn't dare open his eyes.

"Vera." His voice is a warning. My name rumbled over his tongue like an elicit vow he's telling himself.

"Did you think about what you could do to me?" My tone cracks, desire lacing my words. If I can't reason with him, then provoking him is my other option. "Did you imagine opening my legs and touching me there while I was asleep?"

I've barely gotten the words out when

he opens his eyes and grips my neck in one large hand. The roughness of his skin sends goosebumps skittering over my flesh. His eyes are wide, burning into me, searing me with a mere glare.

"If you keep that up, I'll hurt you."

"Will you?" I choke out, testing him when I should be meek and submissive. But that's not who I am. He can see it. There's a fire inside me, a need only he can satiate. His fingers tighten; he's squeezing the breath from me. My body is merely a toy, a rag doll, at his mercy.

Spots appear in my vision as my lungs struggle for air. But Logan doesn't listen, doesn't release me. He smiles, a dark, promising grin that causes me to shiver violently. I've read about breath play, so many times, imagining it, fantasizing about it, but actually having it done is very different.

"Are you wet for me?" he grits out, his teeth clenched as he stares at me. I can't nod. My head is lolling to the side. "Does this make you ache for my cock inside you?" Once again, I can't respond, so I merely watch him through my hooded gaze. My lashes are fluttering, and a lightheaded feeling is slowly taking over.

I'm about to allow it to steal me when Logan releases me, and I stumble backward into the wall. My hands shoot out to grip something, but instead, I slip to my ass, the plush throw rug softening the blow.

I can't believe that just happened. But most of all, I can't believe I really am wet. My panties are soaked, and the pulse between my thighs is thrumming.

"Don't mistake me feeding you, being nice to you, as me being a good man," he tells me, not helping me to my feet. My gaze darts around the room, but it's only when Logan steps closer to me that my eyes land on his crotch. The thickness of him pressing against the zipper of his jeans.

My body shivers at the thought of him pushing that inside me. He doesn't move closer, but he doesn't move away either. The power exchange in the room hangs heavily over us. He's the strong alpha male, and I'm the soft, gentle figurine here for him to play with.

"You're . . ." I don't know what to say. My words taper off into nothing. The silence that follows stretches out, almost as if it's a cat elongating and yawning.

"I'm . . .?" he asks.

"I can't believe you did that."

"No, that's not what you can't believe," he tells me, crouching, so we're eye to eye. "What you can't believe is that you're wet, needy." He smirks. "You can't believe your pretty pussy is pulsing, aching to be filled."

I try to shake my head, but it's pointless because he's right.

"Tell me, Vera," he says, his voice tight, and his body taut with . . . something. Need? I don't know, but he wants to hear me admit it. I open my mouth, but nothing comes out. I wish I could be honest, say what I feel, what I need, but actually saying the words out loud will make it real.

"Leave me alone," I mumble, my throat still burning from the tightness of how he held me. I wonder if I'm bruised. Logan watches me for a long while before he nods and rises. I watch him turn and stride away. He can read me, it's clear. Apparently, to Logan Oakridge, I'm an open book, and all he wants to do is turn the pages until there are no more secrets between us.

But I need to hold onto mine for a moment longer. The door shuts, and I sit there in silence, thinking about what just happened. I want him. It's clear my body responds to him in ways I never expected. And now he knows it too.

I glance up, remembering he brought me dinner. I scoot over to the tray and find a glass of orange soda, along with a plate of pot pie and now-cold fries. Beside it is a bowl; inside, I see a double chocolate cupcake. A small smile tilts my lips, but I catch myself from enjoying the moment.

I settle on the stool, eating slowly, thinking about Logan, and how my mind is awash with images of him doing things to me. I grab a book and flip it open, reading while I eat. Focusing my attention on the words as I savor the peppery flavor of the meat and vegetables on my plate.

Once dinner is finished, I grab the bowl and head to bed. The orange drink I sit on the nightstand as I settle back against the headboard and read a tale of how Sleeping Beauty fell in love with the prince.

The chocolatey goodness of the dessert

makes me moan in pleasure. I've always had a weakness for chocolate, and this is one of the most delicious cakes I've tasted. Once it's finished, I set the bowl on the nightstand and scoot lower under the covers. A chill has come over, and the room isn't as warm as it was when the sun was shining through the windows.

I'm still not sure what the time is, but weariness overtakes me, and soon enough, my eyes are fluttering closed.

CHAPTER FOURTEEN
Logan

I SMILE AS I WATCH HER SLEEP. THE CAMERA sitting in the corner of her room is out of sight, and it allows me to observe my Sleeping Beauty as she dreams. I wonder what is running through her mind right now.

Is she dreaming of me?

When I taunted her earlier, I saw her pupils dilate with every filthy promise I made, and even though I expected her to fight me on it, she didn't.

The feel of her delicate throat in my hold was enough to have my cock aching to be inside her. I've always been more turned on with women who weren't looking at me, who weren't able to fight, to speak while I was inside them. The broken parts of me loved the shattered parts of them. But with Vera, there's something different.

I can't explain it, and I definitely can't define it. Nothing I feel around her makes sense. Not the way I want her to see me while I take her. Not the way her feisty nature makes every inch of my body grow hard and needy. And not even the way I crave to see her come apart.

At almost thirty years old, I shouldn't be sitting here watching her on a small screen while I jerk my dick, but I am. Like a demented fucking stalker, I'm getting off while she's asleep in my bed.

She rolls over, the blanket falling from her body, and I take note of how her smooth, porcelain thighs are splayed. Her panties are tight against her cunt, and the puffy lips are prominent. A groan of pleasure escapes my lips as I feel my release nearing.

I'm almost there. I'm about to find euphoria when she once again moves, and I catch a glimpse of her pert ass. The smooth material offering her up like a sacrifice. She's beautiful, perfect in every way.

I want nothing more than to rub myself

against her ass, to feel her softness, and make her moan while she's asleep. To mark her with my seed while she's oblivious to my pleasure. And when she wakes, she'll feel the stickiness of me all over her.

I smile.

My hand moves faster.

She taunts me unknowingly as she becomes restless.

My hand stops suddenly when she shoots up, screaming into the darkness of the bedroom. I'm on my feet in seconds, shoving my dick into my jeans. Pain causes me to wince as I race up the stairs to unlock her door and shove it open.

Vera is crying on the bed, her body wracked with sobs, and I don't think twice about pulling her into my arms. I'm on the mattress, holding her against me as she cries. I'm not sure what the fuck just happened, but she better tell me the truth, or I'll spank it out of her.

I listen to her cries. The soft, mewling sounds lull her and me into a false sense of security, and soon enough, I feel her fall asleep in my arms. Her body is so small compared to mine. My arms cocoon her, and I feel her heat against me. Vera is nestled in my arms, the soft scent of vanilla still in her hair as I close my eyes and inhale the fragrance.

Her gentle breaths wisp from her slightly parted lips, and I watch her. The golden strands of her hair frame her face. The apples of her cheeks are shaded with a soft pink, and I can't help but take her in.

Would this ever work between us?

How can we ever make this permanent?

The questions circle themselves in my mind as I watch her sleep. She truly is beautiful. My body hums with need when she nestles farther into my hold, and I tighten my arms around her. My cock is straining against my zipper. My earlier pleasure is still apparent.

Her arm slips down, her hand falling against the bulge in my jeans, causing me to hold my breath. She doesn't realize what she's doing. She's asleep, and before I can chastise myself or feel any guilt, I take her hand and press it against the hardness of my cock.

The pulse that thrums in my chest shoots down to my cock, and a groan is drawn from deep in my gut. I know this is wrong. I know this is not keeping her safe, but rather taking advantage, but I can't help myself.

I close my eyes as pure adrenalin zaps through my veins, like an electric shock coursing through me from the top of my head down to my toes. They curl in my socks; the ache only intensifies the harder I press. Her tiny hand is so small compared to my cock. I picture her gripping it, stroking it.

"Fuck," I hiss under my breath as I use her limp hand to jerk me off through the material of my jeans. I should stop, but I don't. I never once claimed to be a good man, and this time it's no different as pleasure seeps from the tip of my cock, wetting my jeans, the damp spot visible through the material.

My body locks and I squeeze her fingers around my shaft, the material causing friction to rub against the smooth flesh, and I come harder than I ever have before. I'm shuddering while holding onto her as if she were my lifeline. A buoy in the middle of an ocean of darkness, and she's my only light. Guiding me to the shore. But I'm afraid — instead of her saving us both, I'll drag us into the depths.

Guilt weighs heavily on me as I make coffee. It's not even six in the morning, and I'm wide awake. Normally, I'd be out for a run, trying to forget the night before, but I didn't want to leave Vera alone. When I went out to the store, I half expected her to have gotten away.

The clouds are gray and heavy as the light of dawn approaches. I sip my coffee on the porch, looking through the heavy tree trunks as I think about what I did last night. The moment I came, I slid out from where Vera was practically curled around me and left her alone.

I needed to clean up, but I also needed space from her. Having her so close, I lost control and did the one thing I never wanted to do to her. I used her as if she were nothing more than a toy. Perhaps she is, but I shouldn't have done it.

I'm stronger than that.

At least, I thought I was.

My chest is tight with anxiety as I think about her waking and seeing her hand pleasuring me. I wanted so badly to offer her the same, but if I did, I would've woken her, and she would've been more afraid of me than she's ever been.

"Logan!" Her screech is enough to have me nearly dropping my mug on the ground. But I hold fast and race inside. Pushing the door open, I find her on the bed, her body shaking and her eyes wide.

"What?" I rush to her side, needing to hold her once more. Even though I should stay far away from her, treat her as I would a stranger who's just staying in my home for a short while, I can't. "What's wrong, Beauty?"

"I . . . I had a bad dream," she mumbles into my shirt and tugs at the material, pulling me closer to her. "I thought . . . I didn't . . . I was dying. I couldn't breathe," she tells me, and my chest tightens with concern I haven't felt in a long while.

"What happened?" I ask her, lowering my voice to an almost-whisper as I take in her shaking form. Her tiny body curls into mine as she holds me. I wonder if she realizes what she's doing. If this were any other day, she would be pushing me away, so this dream must've done a number on her.

"Your dad found me," she finally chokes out through sobs that wrack her body. "I couldn't get away." Her whine does things to me that I should ignore, but I can't stop glancing down at my sweatpants that have a clear bulge slowly appearing.

Fuck.

This girl is messing with my head more and more each day.

"You're safe here," I tell her, knowing he's nowhere near this shithole town. That reminds me. I need to check in on her apartment. The security footage should bring back something. Surely.

If there's one thing I know about Herbert Oakridge, it's that he doesn't fuck around. When he wants something, he doesn't allow anything to stop him.

"Why would you take me? I was safe. I'd almost forgotten about you." Her words slice right through to my very gut. My soul, the one that's so black it's pure fucking charcoal, aches at the thought of me hurting her just like my asshole of a father would.

"I needed you safe."

"But you . . . you can't keep me safe. I mean, why do you want me now?" Her question stills me because I don't know how to answer her honestly.

Am I just obsessed with her?

Or is there something more between us?

CHAPTER FIFTEEN
Vera

He doesn't say anything. He doesn't even move.

The muscles of his shoulders are tense, and I can feel how his hands stiffen around me. I shouldn't have asked him, but I needed to know. If he's keeping me here, if he's so attracted to me, then there must be more between us. I can't be imagining it.

"Logan?"

He moves off the bed and stares out the window, keeping his back to me. The shirt he's wearing is taut against his muscles. I watch as his knuckles whiten with the fist he's made. The tattoos that adorn his hands and forearms are pulsing.

"Logan, please don't shut me out?" I sound so timid, so young that I'm unsure if the voice I hear is mine. He turns to me, and I take in the way the top five buttons of his shirt are undone. The ink that peeks through makes me curious as to what else is there. What's hidden under the material.

I allow myself to take in all the tattoos that cover his body. The colorful artwork makes his tanned skin seem like a canvas—tempting and intriguing. Now that they're clearly on show, I stare at them for a moment longer than I know is friendly. I'm checking him out, and I immediately admonish myself.

"I can't do this with you," he tells me. He rakes his fingers through his hair, tugging at the dark strands. He doesn't have his glasses on, so I can see his eyes clearly. He's still tense, but now when he glances up from under his long black lashes, I see it—fear.

"Why?" I challenge, scooting off the bed and making my way toward him. "Why can't you just be honest with me?" I'm inches from him. The heat emanating off him comes in waves of cedar and oak. He smells like . . . safety.

"Don't do this, Vera." His words are strained, and the pained expression on Logan's face only becomes more prominent. His brows furrow and his body visibly trembles the moment I place my palm on his shoulder.

Heat sears me from the contact between us, and I step one more inch closer, so my body is flush with his. Even though he's not wearing shoes, I'm still almost half his size. The man is like a caveman, tall and broad. He looks down at me, dark eyes swirling with danger and agony.

"Logan, I can't stay here if you're not going to give me the truth." My voice is low, but I'm so close he must feel my words whisper along his jaw.

"I'm . . . I did something last night." The confession falls from his perfectly full lips. "I fucking lost all control with you so close to me, and I can't stop myself anymore." The gaze he pins me with burns me from the inside out. "It felt so good. I've never experienced pleasure like that before."

"Then why is it bad?" I'm genuinely curious.

Logan chuckles, his shoulders shaking as he stares me down. "You need to be scared of me,

Vera. I'm a fucking depraved asshole, and all I can think about is using you. About watching you sleep and toying with you like a limp fucking doll made for my pleasure."

My mouth falls open, but it's from the shock of how my body reacts to his words. I want to step even closer to him. I want to climb into his lap and tell him to do those things to me, but I don't.

Instead, I shut my mouth and press my hand against his chest. Gently, I dance my fingers along his body, up to his shoulders. With my other hand, I do the same, until I'm holding onto him.

Without warning him, I leap into the air, and instinctively, he grabs my ass and holds me there. I feel powerful, knowing how much I affect him. All these years, I thought I wasn't worthy of him when it was just our age difference that had pushed him away. I don't blame him. I used to, but now that I know it was *me* but the fact that his father was sick enough to think Logan would want me when I was a child.

"Tell me all the things you want to do to me," I plead, pressing my lips against his. It's a mere brush of our mouths, but I feel his fingers dig into the fleshy globes of my butt. "Tell me, Logan. I want to know it all. I want to look inside you and see what you're hiding." I don't know where the words come from, but they're a plea for more.

"Why aren't you running?" he asks, his voice pained. The expression on his handsome, rugged face is filled with confusion at what I can possibly see in him. How can I possibly *want* to stay here? I've lost my mind, but I shrug it off.

"I can't run. You made it clear," I tell him. "Also, you're the only one who's ever truly *wanted* me. You . . . understand my mind, the darkness that seems to live there on a daily basis."

"Is this about the fantasies you confessed online?"

I nod.

"And you want that with me?" he questions incredulously.

"I trust you, more than anyone else I know in my life. Why can't you see that you're not truly bad? You're just broken, and you're living with guilt."

Logan stares at me for a long time, and I'm sure he's about to throw me on the bed and tell me to leave him alone, but he doesn't. He turns, settling me on the mattress before he heads toward the door.

"Wait! Where are you going?" I ask, my chest tightening at the thought of him locking me in here again without anyone to talk to. I can only imagine he's lonely, living up here with nothing but trees for company.

"I need time to think."

"And you're just leaving me in here?" My question is filled with a plea that's clear and evident. My heart thuds against my ribs. It's painful, but I ignore the ache. I want to run to him and ask him not to leave me, but I don't. I'm not going to beg him if he's made up his mind.

"For now." He shuts the door behind him with a thud, and I sit and stare at the wooden object for a long while after he leaves.

When the door finally opens again after a

few hours, I can only tell because the sky has changed color. Logan saunters in with a tray filled with food. A plate of lasagna with salad on the side. He's also included a bowl of what looks like chocolate cupcakes that have been cut into smaller pieces.

"I thought you'd be hungry," he tells me with a grin. "Earlier," he starts, "I was caught off guard by your words. I didn't expect you to say something like that."

"I . . . I wasn't expecting what I said either," I tell him honestly. It's true. I was so shocked by my pleas that I sat for a long while, reconsidering what I said.

"Did you mean it?" he asks, sounding like a little boy scared of what I could say. He is lonely. I notice it in his gaze when he looks at me right now. A man so strong, so powerful, yet he's as broken as I am. I guess nobody can overcome loneliness. And not everyone is what you're expecting from a mere glance.

"I did." I nod the words no longer a lie. I'm not here to try to force him to let me go. If he needs me here to keep me safe, I'm going to trust him just like he's trusting me with his confessions.

"I'm not sure about this." He sounds lost to the thoughts that must be dancing in his mind. "I'm not gentle. I'm not a fucking sweet and loving man," he tells me earnestly, and I can't help but smile. "There are things that . . . I haven't told you."

My heart stills at his words, but I don't back down. "Then tell me now."

He pins me with a pained glare, one filled with so much agony it steals the breath from my lungs. I want to hold him. I want to wrap my arms around him and keep all those pieces of him together. To stop him from falling to tiny fragments at my feet. But I don't move. I wait, holding my breath, watching the way his eyes burn with the past demons he's fighting.

"I don't know how to do this," he tells me. "To be a man with a woman by his side." The truth spills from his lips like a cool drink of water. As if quenching my thirst, he continues, "I've been taught to be cold, brutal, savage."

"But that's not who you are deep down," I insist. I can see he's at war with himself from the way his shoulders tense to the way his jaw ticks as he grinds his teeth together.

"The thing is," he tells me, a wry tilt of his lips making his face darken even though it's an attempt at a smile. "I've always thought I was broken. Cursed by something. And when I look back at my childhood, I realize I am. My father is not a good man. He never was. But all I know, I learned from him."

"Did he . . .? I mean . . . was he . . .?"

"Did he abuse me?" he questions, and I nod. "No. Never. He was . . . oblivious to me until I turned eighteen and had to meet my future bride." Logan pins me with a stare. It was the day he saw me for the first time.

"Something must have happened after you walked out that day at my birthday party," I voice my theory, and he nods. I'm right. "He did something, said something to you." My chest tightens when Logan sighs and pushes away from me. He stalks toward the window, leaving me shivering from the cold he's left behind.

He keeps his back to me as he stares out at the now-fading light. The large frame of him blocks out most of the view, but I don't go to him. I realize he needs to come to terms with whatever he's going to tell me.

"We went home. He didn't speak to me at all. The moment I stepped foot inside the house, he left me to head to his office. He ignored me for the rest of the day until I finally built up the courage to go to him. It was only when I got to his library, which I was never allowed to enter, that I heard him speaking."

He's quiet for a long while, so I ask, "What did he say?"

"I don't know who he was talking to, but I know it was a woman. I heard her voice. She was the one who told him I'm broken. I'd never heard her voice before, she was a stranger to me, yet she knew me inside out. As if she'd shoved her hand into my gut and touched my soul."

"I don't understand." I fold my arms across my chest as the chill seeps through my clothes, taking root in the marrow of my bones.

"It all sounds so far-fetched," Logan says as he chuckles. "But she said I would always crave darkness. That I was born with it, but only when I turned eighteen would I truly know what it means. My birthday was the day before; she didn't realize she was warning him a day late."

CHAPTER SIXTEEN
Logan

I RECALL EVERY MOMENT OF THAT NIGHT. THE woman who sounded like a witch sending out a curse into the world for me chilled me to the bone. She was there for a reason, and I never learned who she was. My father never told me about it, and I never asked. I wanted to, but I knew he wouldn't offer me the truth.

"What do you mean?" Dad's voice is cold, filled with ice, and drenched in poison. I've heard him angry before, but this is something else. I can't see his face, but I can certainly picture how it's screwed up with anger.

"He is going to find the darkness that resides inside him," she speaks again. My body is rigid

with fear, with a violent cold that's threaded through my veins. "And when he does, he'll never find true happiness."

"He walked away from her. I couldn't stop him." My father's voice is urgent as if he's trying to convince himself and her of what I did today.

Silence greets me, and I'm tempted to push the door open, but I can't. If I do, he'll hear me, see me, and then I'll be in worse trouble than I am right now. I know I should've stayed and spoken to the girl. But how can my father expect me to want her?

"Don't put this on him," my father pleads. "If anything, let him go from this stupidity."

"This is on you," the woman says. "He will spend his life alone. Broken. His soul, which was once light and carefree, will be tainted with the darkness that you hold in your bloodline."

"No!" The roar of the word rumbles through the walls, and it doesn't take long for it to hit me right in the chest. "You will not do this to him."

"It is done, Oakridge," she responds quickly "You know I can ruin you with the information I have."

"What happened then?" Vera's soft, innocent

tone drags me from the horrid memory, causing me to turn around and finally face her.

"It didn't happen overnight, but slowly, with every girl I spent time with, it never worked. I didn't understand it, but then, when the woman I was last with saw my true desires, that's when I realized that it's true—my soul is black, stained with needs nobody could ever cure me of."

"But you're not evil, Logan. You're not your father, and this—" she waves her hand in the air while shaking her head in disbelief — "curse, is bullshit."

"It's not bullshit," I bite out. "I've lived with it for most of my adult life and . . ." Shaking my head, I turn away from her again, not needing to see how she's watching me right now. It makes me feel like I can be *that* man for her, and I know I can't. "I can't change who I am."

"I'm not asking you to change. I'm asking you to give this a chance."

Spinning on my heel, I step up to Vera, looming over her smaller frame. I engulf every part of her. I'm larger, I'm stronger, and I could so easily take her and hide her away. I have, but not the way I'd like. Where she can't find anything other than me in her life. When I'm the one she needs, the one she craves when she thinks about her darkest desires. I've wanted that for two long years, and now that she's here, my restraint is taut, ready to snap.

"You want this?" I ask, quirking a brow as I gesture with my chin around the room. "I *stole* you, Vera. I'm no fucking prince."

"No, you're not royalty, and yes, you kidnapped me, held me in this godforsaken cabin for I don't know how long, but you're doing it to keep me safe." Her words are confident. She's not lying. I did this to keep her safe from the asshole, who is my dear father. But I also wanted her for myself.

"You're as fucked up as I am," I tell her with a chuckle.

She shrugs, offering me a smile. "I know." I expect her to walk away, but she doesn't. Her eyes lock on mine, and she steps that one inch closer to me, and the air in the room disappears. Every molecule in my body is sparking as if electricity is shooting through me. It feels like I've been struck by a fucking lightning bolt. "But that's what makes us perfect for each other."

"I can't . . . I mean . . ."

"I don't want normal, I want . . ." She looks up at me, smiling, the mischievous glint in her eyes telling me I don't need to worry. Her demons that seem to hide under the innocent exterior look like they want to play with mine. "You."

I can't take it anymore. I crash my mouth to hers, our lips molding together. The heat of her makes me shudder with need. I grasp her face in my hands, holding her at an angle so my tongue can dip into her mouth.

The flavor of her is like nothing I've ever tasted. No other woman that I've ever kissed has made my body react the way she does. Our kiss deepens, as my hands trail down over her shoulders toward her hips, and I grip her, tugging her closer to me until there's no longer space between us.

Nothing in this world exists except us and this moment. I lose myself to it. My eyes are closed, but it's like I can see her expression. She's emblazoned in my mind. Burnt in my heart since the day I realized I made a mistake by walking away from her.

Vera whimpers and I steal it with that kiss until I feel dizzy from it. She's intoxicating, more so than any drug, any alcohol I've ever tasted. When I finally pull away from her, I watch her lashes flutter, and then I'm met with those mirror-like eyes. I can see myself in her gaze, but it's not the person I always see when I look in the mirror. This time, I'm different. I'm *good*.

"I want you on the bed," I tell her. "Lie back, close your eyes, and just don't move."

She looks at me, her eyes wide with wonder, and I can't imagine what scenarios are going through her mind. With a nod, she moves toward the bed, and I watch her slip onto the mattress, her body languid and calm.

Her obedience makes my body shiver. My cock isn't completely hard, but the stirrings of desire are there. It's been such a long time since I've felt that familiar ache while watching a woman move. It shocks me.

Once Vera is on her back, her eyes close, and she looks like she's sleeping. I've never done this with someone before, and my stomach is tight with anxiety. It coils in my gut, swirling around like a snake ready for the attack.

I take a few tentative steps, and when I finally reach the bed, I stop. I can't bring myself to move. But Vera is so obedient. She doesn't open her eyes, doesn't speak, and at times, I wonder if she's even breathing.

My jeans get tighter. The way she's just lying there, helpless, unsure of my next move, it makes my dick hard. The throb is familiar, and I can't help but touch myself through the material.

She's so beautiful.

My Sleeping Beauty.

I reach for her. My fingertips tentatively touching the smoothness of her arm. The silkiness of her skin is enough to send me into blind need. But I need to be careful. She's not only fragile, she's someone who's accepting this, accepting me.

Gently, I trail my touch down to her wrist, where I feel the thrumming of her heartbeat. The only thing, other than her breathing that tells me she's alive. My cock is harder than steel, attempting to fight its way from my jeans, but I don't make a move to take it out to stroke myself.

Instead, I revel in her body, noticing how her nipples harden and pebble against the material of her tank top. A slight whimper falls free from her plump lips, but I don't stop. I continue my ministrations, tweaking the buds gently. Vera's sounds come more frequently. A moan, a mewl, but I can't stop. I'm lost to the pleasure I'm bestowing on her body.

"Please don't," I plead with her when I notice she's going to open her eyes. I want this so badly that I'm trying not to lose all my control. She doesn't look at me, and I smile down at her. Like a puppet for me to toy with, I reach the apex of her creamy thighs and gently press against her mound, feeling her warmth.

My fingers dance along her body, all the way up, and all the way back down until her hips are moving of their own volition. Even though I know she's not really sleeping, she's playing the part well.

More moans fall free from her lips, and I lean in to press my mouth to hers. The heat, the contact sizzles, and soon enough, I'm licking into her warmth, tasting her once more and like a drug. My body prickles from head to toe, wanting another hit, and another.

Her eyes snap open when I pull away, my hand leaving her body, my mouth unlocking from hers. Those beautiful eyes that shimmer like jewels in the sunshine meet mine. For a long moment, I'm sure she's about to tell me to let her go, to leave her the fuck alone because I'm a perverse psychopath, but she doesn't. Instead, she whispers, "I want more."

CHAPTER SEVENTEEN
Vera

HE STARES AT ME.

He doesn't move. I'm sure he's not even breathing as he watches me. I can't believe how wet I am. I'm turned on, more than I've ever been before. No matter the strangeness of the situation, I crave it—what he has to offer.

He slowly moves closer, and I know this is new to him, being with someone while they're awake, but I take it upon myself to reach for him. My hand grazes over the thick denim material, feeling his rigidness behind the zipper.

"I can't, Vera," he tells me, his voice taut with emotion. There's a strain in his expression, creasing his ruggedly handsome face. "I just can't. Not yet." *Not yet.* That's all I needed to know. And the more I touch him, the softer he gets, and I realize it's because my eyes are on him. As if he's worried about me seeing him like that, in a state of pleasure.

"Have you ever touched yourself for a girl?" I ask the question that's suddenly burst into my mind. I don't know why I think it, but for some reason, I think he's convinced himself that if he was with someone, naked, he'd be vulnerable. And the fear of that has taken hold of him.

Not some stupid curse.

But his own mindset.

"No," he grits out as I continue trailing my fingers over his body. Every hard ridge of muscle on his stomach, the way his hips taper from the broadness of his shoulders makes me want to explore him.

"I want to try something," I tell him. "Will you allow me to?" He nods slowly, his dark gaze locked on mine. He doesn't look at my hands moving over him, and I slowly unbutton his plaid shirt, pushing it over his shoulders. The material falls to the floor, and he's now bared to me. The ink that adorns his chest is a colorful canvas of artwork which I tentatively touch.

The smoothness of his skin under my fingers causes sparks to shoot through me. He doesn't make a move to stop me, so I lean in farther and plant a kiss to his left pectoral muscle, then the right. My mouth flutters over his torso down toward his stomach, where I do what I've been dying to. I trace the dips of his abs with my tongue.

A growl vibrates through him at the cool wetness of me. When I reach the waistband of his jeans, I move quickly to undo the belt buckle, then the button and zipper before pushing the material down. His boxer briefs are dark blue, and I tug at them until they're at his thick thighs.

I don't look at him when I take his heavy cock in my hand and slowly stroke it. I close my eyes, focusing on the task at hand, and I lie so still, holding my breath, which seems to work because I feel the twitch in his shaft and the smooth, velvety flesh slowly hardens in my palm.

"Vera," Logan growls, low and demanding. I ignore him and continue taunting him, seducing him. I'm new to this, unsure of what I'm doing, but I know I'm having the desired effect on him because seconds later, Logan's fingers tangle in my hair as he tugs my head back. "I'm going to hurt you." His pained words fall around me, surrounding me in the darkness, he's promising.

Logan pushes me back onto the bed, and in a flash of movement, he's hovering over me. His body taut with unrestrained desire. His cock nudges my core, causing me to whimper at the thought of him inside me.

"Do you want that?" he growls over my lips, his mouth brushing along mine, and the heat of his breath wafts over me. He's all darkness and sin, and I drink him in, the broken man that's mine. I realize in that moment Logan Oakridge is mine.

I nod.

I nod with all I have and all that I am because I do want it.

His large hand wraps around the slender column of my neck, and he squeezes. The way his fingers dig into the sides of my neck cuts off my breathing. My lungs work hard, but they can't pull in much-needed air.

Dark eyes burn into me. Stars dot my vision. My lips part and Logan steals them, kissing me hard and furious. His tongue licks along my lower lip before he pulls it into his mouth and bites down hard on the plump flesh.

A mewl of pained agony tumbles from my mouth to his, and he swallows it just like he's taking my breath. He doesn't release me when he reaches between us and circles my clit with his fingers. The taunting, teasing touch of his fingers graze over me, sending spirals of white-hot pleasure burning through me from the top of my head to the tips of my toes.

Pain and pleasure swirl together in the darkness as I feel myself falling into the abyss, but I don't fight him. I allow him to give me pleasure while taking his own, and just as my eyes fall closed and I no longer see him before me, a wave of pure, unfiltered pleasure shoots through me so violently I shudder and shake beneath him, and the heat of his orgasm splashes against my skin.

That's the last thing I feel before I finally pass out.

My eyes open to warmth holding me

hostage. It's only when I attempt to roll over that I realize I can't. There's a heavy arm draped over me. A large hand is cupping my breast, holding me against a hard, muscled body.

"I'm sorry," Logan whispers. "I lost control. I hurt you, and I'm just so fucking sorry." His words wash over me as the memory returns. He held me down, he made me come, and I passed out from the orgasm.

"You didn't hurt me," I tell him, but I can't see his expression because my back is cocooned to his front. "I was just overwhelmed by the orgasm."

"Don't fucking make excuses for me," he grits out. He's angry, but it's all at himself, not me. "I should never have tried this." There's so much agony in his voice; it makes my chest tighten painfully.

"I'm not making excuses, Logan. I asked you for more, and you gave it to me. I wanted it," I insist. "Nothing you did hurt me." I force myself to roll over, and I finally come face to face with him. The guilt is written all over his face. He's looking at me with so much sadness my heart thuds against my ribs.

"It will never happen again," he tells me before pressing a gentle kiss to my forehead, and then he pushes off the bed and heads for the door.

"Wait! Where are you going?"

He doesn't turn around. Instead, he grips the door handle and twists it, pulling the door open and walking out into the hallway. "Time for me to finish this so I can send you home, and you can live your life like I knew you should—without me." And then he shuts the door with a loud bang, and suddenly I'm all alone.

My eyes fill with tears when I realize he's going to leave me. For one short moment, I thought we could do this, be together, perhaps find happiness with each other. Our desires run alongside each other so well. What I crave, he can deliver, but what he needs is something *he* doesn't believe I can give him. And because of that, he thinks that walking away from me is the best option.

I'm not sure what he means by finishing something, but I have the distinct feeling he's about to start a war with his father. That doesn't bode well for either of us.

Herbert Oakridge is two things—dangerous and connected—which will only ensure he makes an example of me and his son.

Sighing, I push off the bed and pad over to the door to find it locked. He's keeping me captive once more. After all the progress I made with him, we're back to square one. I should never have done what I did, but I don't regret it.

I can't lose Logan. I'm not sure why I'm so invested in him. Perhaps it's because he understands me. Nobody ever has. All my life was lived with the acceptance that I was a good girl who behaved, but deep down, there was always another layer to my personality. A darker version of me. And now that Logan has brought it out of me, I can't hide her any longer.

"Logan," I call to him, but I don't hear his movements on the other side. He may be downstairs, but I don't stop my speech. "I know you're angry with yourself for what happened, but I'm not. Don't I get a say in what happens in my life? I thought you were different from your father, but the way you're acting, you're turning into him."

I wait, but he still doesn't make me aware

of where he is or if he's even listening to me. My heart pounds against my chest, and I fist my hands and bang them against the wooden door.

"You're not him. Please don't do this, Logan! You're nothing like him. Our journey may not be a perfect fairy tale, but you can change our story." My voice is lower now, hope slowly ebbing away from me. I can't get through to him if he's not allowing me to talk to him, if he's not listening.

I close my eyes and breathe deeply. The guilt of what I did, how I pushed him, is at the forefront of my mind. Even though I craved what he did, aching for his violence, I should've taken it slower. But pleasure had taken hold of me, and I didn't want to stop because I believed he could handle it.

I was wrong.

So damn wrong.

"Logan don't send me away," I plead this time. I'm not screaming, I'm not shouting. My voice is low, a pained plea, hoping he can hear me from wherever he is in the house.

CHAPTER EIGHTEEN
Logan

Ilean my head against the door. My palm flat against the wood, as if I can feel her through the thickness of it. I know she's right on the other side. My body aches to be near her. She's done something to me, broken through walls I've built and burrowed herself inside me.

Over the past week, all I've wanted was to feel her, to touch her like I did last night, and then I ended up hurting her. She can deny it all she wants, but I know what I did. Losing control like that has guilt weighing me down. My gut is heavy with the dark emotion that's eaten away at me over the years.

Vera isn't like other girls. That's a fact. But I can't be near her if she allows me to do what

I did last night. She passed out and seeing her limp body was an aphrodisiac, which is why I need to send her away. It's wrong on so many levels. I shouldn't *want* her like that, but I do.

I thought I could be normal when she tasted me. The moment her delicate hand wrapped around my dick, and I watched her lie down, eyes closed, I hardened again, and I thought it would work, but the more I craved her, the worse my control got.

I snapped.

I shouldn't have.

"Logan, I want you to do it again," she speaks up again. "I want you to hold me down on the bed, touch me while I sleep. I want you to find pleasure with me. I'm not afraid of you."

I want nothing more than to do what she asks. I want to storm into the room, hold her, keep her, but I know she doesn't deserve this life. My mind is a mess, torn between doing the right thing and taking what I crave to own.

I move down the stairs until I reach my phone. No messages. I hit dial on the number I should've called yesterday. I want to tell my father that he can't have her, that she's no longer his to take.

I settle in the chair, hitting the display of the cameras, and before my contact can answer the phone, I kill the call to stare at the screen before me. He found her apartment. Thankfully, they can't track her here. He won't know where she's gone. I made sure her computer, phone, and iPad were all offline before coming here, so there's no way for him to find us.

To find her.

Silence from above greets me, and I hope she's finally asleep. My gut churns with the guilt of what I did. I made a mistake, the reminder of that is clear in my mind. I should never have touched her. Watching her body go limp, waking her back up, and then watching her slide into a dreamless sleep beside me was what I clearly needed to make the decision.

I'm going to face my father. It's been years, and I ran for good reason, but now I'm going to return for an even better one. I want to fix myself, mend the brokenness about me so I can give her what she needs.

Every thought I have of walking away from here burns me from the inside out. I can't watch her leave, and I can't send her away. Even though I know, I should. I can't love her, but I can make sure she's safe and happy.

My phone rings, dragging me out of the moral dilemma I'm going through, and I see Dax's number on display. Swiping the screen to answer, I press the phone to my ear.

"What's up?"

"He's on the warpath," Dax tells me, no greeting, straight to business. "I doubt he's going to give up any time soon. Are you sure you're well hidden because I have a feeling that he's pulling out all the stops with this?" His tone is urgent, which only seems to make my stomach twist into a tighter knot than it's been in for a long while.

"I am. She's . . . she's with me, and I'm not prepared to let her go," I tell him. "I can't let her go."

"I have other news as well," he speaks. His voice is controlled, tone calm and collected, but I have a feeling what he's about to tell me is far from it. But I'm met with silence. I pull the phone away, checking to see if the call is still connected. It is.

"Dax?"

"It's your mother," he tells me, causing my body to grow stiff, tense with fear that my father has killed her, or worse, maimed her and tortured her. "She's gone. We're not sure where. I have my men working on tracking her, but he's not giving anything away."

I think about the times she called me, and I ignored her. I should've answered. I wasn't a good son, not one to spend time with her, or even sit and talk to her, but I loved her, nonetheless. I think when I finally realized how precious life was, it was too late for me to ever make amends.

"I need her found, or I'll find my father and kill him."

"It will be easier said than done. He's upped his security. Nobody is coming within a few feet of him except the whores he's hiring on a daily basis." Dax's words are laced with disgust. "He was in the club last night," he tells me. Dax owns a club called Inferno, where he has dancers on stage and private rooms just for those with enough cash to throw at the beauties who work there. The difference between Dax and my father is that Dax is a good man. He looks after his girls, giving them a sanctuary from their pasts.

"Was he alone?"

"He had two girls hanging off his arms, but he didn't go into any of the private areas. Met with another man, not sure of his name yet. I'm having Theia go through the sign-ins from last night. Once we have a name, I can send men in to question him."

"Thanks for doing this, man," I tell him. It's been a long time since I've seen Dax. After going into hiding, I didn't want to be found, and heading back to the city would just make matters worse. So, I've kept in touch with Dax through calls, emails, and yet, at times, I wonder why he's still stuck with me for so long.

"You know I'm only a call away. And to be honest, I hate assholes like your father."

I have to agree with him. "Me too."

The story of Dax and his submissive, Theia, would make anyone's skin crawl. Her father was an asshole of note. When they took him down, there was a lot of pain and heartache, not because she missed her dad, but because she found out what he did to the family, to her mother.

"I'll find your mother; my men are working on this twenty-four seven."

"I'm thinking of coming to you, leaving Vera here. She'll be safe, and he won't know where to look. I can't stay here when I know my mom is out there somewhere. What if he's hurt her?"

"You can't risk being seen, Logan." I know Dax is right, but with my mother gone, the game has changed. If something happens to her, it will be on me, and that's not something I could ever live with. Even though I wasn't the best son in the world, she was my anchor, and if Herbert has done anything to her, I'll fucking kill him.

"I can't risk my mother getting hurt because he's angry with me," I tell Dax.

He's silent for a long while, then sighs. "Listen to me. He can just as easily kill you the moment you step foot in the city." He's right, I know he is, but I could never forgive myself for it if I didn't try.

"I'll think about it." My voice is hoarse, my throat dry. I can't think of a worse fate than seeing my father again, but I'm stronger. I'm more volatile than the boy he once knew.

"Talk soon," Dax tells me before hanging up. I sit back, staring out the window overlooking the forest. Being locked away in the middle of nowhere has its perks. But deep down, all I want is for Vera to be safe, to be with me. The last thought glares at me, spinning in my mind. I want her, and I know she wants me. She's made it clear. Even after what I just did to her last night, she tried to convince me I'm not a monster.

Can this truly work?

Is she the one who's supposed to be mine? To cure me.

A knock on the door upstairs jolts me into action. It's time I made sure I can trust her. I'll give her an inch of freedom, and if she takes advantage, I'll know she needs to be locked up.

It's difficult to let go, to allow someone inside when all your life you've spent it hidden in shadows. Alone. I've been lonely for so long, it feels strange to have someone here, to have company. Someone to talk to.

I stand before heading up the steps and stopping just outside her door. She knocks again, and I lay my hand on the cool wood. Can she feel me? I wonder.

"Logan?" Vera calls my name, and every nerve in my body sparks to life. "Logan, I need the bathroom," she pleads and my heart twists. The sincerity in her tone, the way she speaks does things to me. It tears and rips at the darkness molding around me and flicks light back and forth in my mind.

She's everything good in this world.

And me… I'm everything bad.

But like the saying goes, you need balance to exist.

CHAPTER NINETEEN
Vera

The door opens, and Logan stands there looking tired. He hasn't slept, I can tell by the way those dark circles under his eyes seem more prominent now than they did yesterday. The sun hasn't risen, and he's still dressed in the clothes he had on when he left my room.

"You know where the bathroom is," he tells me before turning and making his way back down the steps. My mouth falls open, but no words come out. He's trusting me to be up here alone, not locked up.

Has something changed?

Is he feeling guilty because of what happened?

Shaking my head, I pad over to the bathroom

and shut the door. I try not to consider what could've transpired as I relieve myself and then wash my hands. When I look at my reflection, I don't recognize the woman staring back at me. I feel *different.* But I'm not sure how it happened.

Was it what happened earlier?

I pull open the bathroom door and step out into the hallway. Taking note of the doors, I find mine still open, and another one in the far corner shut tight. But I don't go to it; instead, I head downstairs where I find Logan sitting at the kitchen counter looking at his laptop.

"Am I… Am I in trouble?" I venture deeper into the large open plan space. The living room is homely, with a couch that looks like it's seen better days and a throw rug that matches the one in my room. No tv, no sound system, nothing else but the small wooden coffee table and the sofa.

"I decided that if you're going to be here, I need to trust you," he tells me. He shuts the laptop lid before meeting my questioning gaze. "And I need you to trust me."

"So, I'm no longer a prisoner?" I smile, hoping he'll notice the humor behind my words.

I don't want to make him angry.

It takes a while before he chuckles. "No, you never were a prisoner, I just needed you to hear me out." His voice is gruff as if he's just woken up from a deep sleep.

"After our… I mean, after we…" My words fail me in the moment I need them most. "I meant what I said, Logan."

He tips his head to the side, his dark eyes regard me in silence before he finally asks, "What you said?"

I nod. "I want this, I… I've always thought about you. For a long time, I hated you. It was anger that took over, and I blamed you for walking away and leaving me to be bartered off to your father."

I don't know if this is the best time to be confessing everything, but if he's allowing me out of the room, he needs to know how I feel. What I feel.

"I wanted to hurt you to… I don't know, just hit you and make you feel the pain I did. My heart hurt, Logan." This time, there's a flash of guilt in his stare, before he shakes his head and turns away from me.

"I never meant to hurt you. But you could understand how I felt when my father brought me to your house."

"I do. Now I do, back then, I didn't understand." I settle on the stool opposite him and clasp my hands on the countertop. He takes my fist in his larger hands and holds them tight.

"I never wanted to be like him, to take without consent. It's how my father made his business successful. He stole, he broke the rules, and he hurt people without a second thought."

Agony laces Logan's words, and I wonder what it would've been like to grow up in a world like that. With a father who was so evil, so vile.

"I'm sorry you dealt with that," I tell him. "I… I guess I was lucky, my dad was mostly a good man."

"He is a good man. He's not dead, Vera," Logan is adamant as he speaks. "I'm sorry for stealing you, kidnapping you." He lifts his gaze to mine, sincerity shines in his eyes, and I nod.

"I know you are." The heat of his hands warms me, both inside and out. Affection isn't something I'm used to, and I have a feeling that Logan isn't someone who offers it to just anyone. At least, he doesn't look like a man who can be gentle.

"What are you thinking?" he asks as if he's trying to read my mind.

I shake my head, dropping my gaze to our connection, and I hope I come across unaffected by my mind playing dirty scenarios on a loop. "Nothing," I tell him, but I can feel my cheeks heating from the lie.

"It has nothing to do with what happened earlier?" he questions, causing me to look up at him again. "Tell me, Vera. I was so afraid I hurt you."

"You didn't. I would've told you if you did." He doesn't seem convinced, so I pull away from him, slipping off the seat to round the counter until I'm beside him. I lean in and allow my lips to brush against his cheek. The stubble tickling me as I press a kiss on him.

"Fuck," he mumbles out the curse word. "You do things to me, Beauty," he tells me.

"What things?" I want to coax all his secrets from him. I want to learn who the man beneath this cold exterior is. "Tell me the things I do to you, Logan because I'm sure that they're the same things you do to me."

Silence hangs between us, like a heavy storm cloud. There are sordid secrets that I know he's hiding. If I had to be honest, I am hiding my own. My fantasies may run differently than most women's, but with Logan, I am sure I can finally realize them and not feel ashamed.

"Nobody has ever understood my needs," he finally whispers, breaking through my thoughts. "I was convinced that I would be alone forever, and I was okay with that. I had come to terms with it."

My heart aches in my chest at his admission. I felt the same for a long time. I told myself that I could never have a man in my life who could make me feel the way I needed sexually. My craving for force, for the helpless feeling, isn't something that everyone would be willing to attempt or to even discuss.

"I know what you mean," I tell him. "I was on that website because I needed an outlet."

Logan snaps his gaze to mine, his hands find purchase on my hips, and he pulls me between his thick, muscled thighs. We don't speak, we just stay there, silent in the darkness.

"You make the crazy inside me less intense," he tells me. "Since the first moment I stood in that meadow with you, I felt it. This strange calm took over me, and I couldn't let it go."

I nod slowly before placing my hands on his shoulders. "Then don't send me away, Logan. Don't push me away," I tell him. "I'm not running. I'm not afraid of you."

"You should be."

"Well then call my stupid because I'm not," I retort hotly, and for a moment, I think I've upset him, but then he laughs. The sound so foreign, yet it speaks directly to my heart.

"Let's go to bed," he finally says before scooping me up and taking me to the bedroom door that I noticed was shut earlier. He allows me to reach for the door handle and twist it.

When he steps inside, I notice how manly the room is. With black curtains and bedding, a dark brown throw rug. There aren't any feminine touches to the space, not like my room has.

"Are you okay to stay here with me?" he questions as he sets me on my feet. "You don't have—"

CHAPTER TWENTY
Logan

I't's been a couple of days. She's steered clear of me, except for food and coffee. Vera has sat on the couch a few times reading, and I could feel her eyes on me. I decide today I'm going to attempt a normal conversation with her.

When I hear feet padding down the steps in the mid-morning, I know Vera is awake. It doesn't take her long to reach me where I'm perched at the kitchen counter.

"Good morning," she says before she plants a kiss on my cheek before making her way to the cabinet to grab a mug.

Most of the cupboards don't have doors, so it's easy to find anything in the kitchen. I take note that she's wearing one of my T-shirts, with no pants. Her long, lithe legs look good enough to spread and devour, but I turn my attention on my work. I can't do this, not just yet. I need to focus.

"You look perky this morning," I remark as she sets herself on the stool opposite me where she sat last night.

"I feel like things are about to change, for the better," she tells me with a smile that lights up the whole fucking cabin. "I mean, once we get the jump on your dad and stuff." She looks so innocent as she leans on her elbows, holding her cup and sipping the hot coffee. The tee she's wearing slips off her shoulder, and I take in the smooth, creaminess that peeks at me.

"You wearing my clothes now?" I question, arching a brow at her.

"Yeah, well, I don't have much here since you didn't really pack a lot for me." She shrugs nonchalantly, and I can't help but chuckle. "I like the cabin," she says suddenly, stilling me.

"You do?" I wouldn't have guessed she'd like this place. For me, it's heaven, but for a girl who grew up in a city like Chicago, I would've thought she would prefer the hustle and bustle.

Even though I found her in Pine Lake, I thought that was because she was hiding out, not because she liked it there.

"I've never been a lover of crowds," Vera confesses, dropping her gaze to the mug. "I feel like I was born into the wrong family, into the wrong life."

"Don't say that."

"Why?" She looks up at me, curiosity burning in her pretty eyes that are framed by long dark lashes.

"Because then I would never have found you," I tell her honestly.

Vera straightens in the chair, shock evident in her expression. "Are you being romantic, Logan Oakridge?"

"I don't do romance, Beauty," I admit easily. "I'm not the *good for you* prince, I'm the dragon that will devour you whole." Even as I say it, I realize that she knows it, and she's still here, sitting across from me while wearing my T-shirt that looks so good on her.

"Who said the princess wanted the prince anyway?" She smiles as she takes another sip of her drink. This girl is going to be the end of me.

"I'm heading to the store later. Do you want anything in particular?" I push off the chair and grab a notepad and pen. "Write whatever you want on here, and I'll make sure to get it."

"Can't I come with you?"

Shaking my head, I meet her gaze. "It's too dangerous. If we're both spotted, we would both be in danger."

Vera pouts, her lips pursed, and my dick takes notice of how plump they are. The soft pink color making me pulse with need.

"Fine," she responds while picking up the pen and scribbling down a few items while I watch her. Even though she's aware of me, she doesn't look up, instead she focuses on the page in front of her.

It feels so normal to be here with her. As if we were a proper couple, living together, and I'm heading out to do the shopping while she stays home to do whatever it is women do.

I don't notice her finish up the list because she asks, "What's wrong?" It drags me from my thoughts, bringing me back to the present.

"Nothing."

"Logan, do you think we could ever be like

this in a normal situation?" she asks in response.

"What?"

"I don't know. I mean, we're like a couple. Right?" This time when she looks at me, I see it in her eyes. She cares, or something. She has feelings for me even after I kidnapped her.

"Vera," I mumble her name as I consider what this could mean.

"No, please don't tell me I'm being stupid."

I turn away, focusing on the truck outside instead of looking at her. "I'm not going to tell you anything that's a lie." I grip the counter so hard, my knuckles turn white. I want nothing more than to believe we can make this work, but I'm not into fairy tales. My story doesn't end with a happily ever after.

"Logan," she calls to me, but I can't look at her. "Please, Logan, tell me you feel it. You have to." Her plea twists my gut.

"Vera," I say her name once more, then spin on my heel to look at her. "I feel every fucking thing that you do. I want nothing more than to claim you as mine. To keep you locked away in a tower where nobody can find you."

"Which is pretty much what you did," she

tells me on a shrug.

"Fuck." I run my fingers through my hair, tugging the strands, pulling so hard, I feel the bite of pain as it pricks my scalp. "I never meant to hurt you. To steal you."

"I know." She's in front of me in seconds, her hands on my arm, but I can't touch her because I'm craving her far too much. "I'm going to the store." I pull away from her, grabbing her scribbled list and my wallet. I don't lock her in, I don't even tell her not to leave, I make my way to the truck before I race back inside and take her the way I want to.

It's better that I go get something for dinner and perhaps a bottle of wine. I've never been big on drinking, but maybe I can show her a small ounce of romance. We could sit and eat together, enjoy some wine, and finally get to know each other.

That's what I want to do, learn about who she is. Deep down, I know that the physical part of a relationship, or whatever we're doing here will take longer to nurture.

Her admission of wanting me, even after what I did shocked me. I knew she enjoyed a few kinks that weren't normal, but I've never seen desire swim in someone's gaze the way it did when I squeezed her neck. When I stole her breath and enjoyed her body.

It's wrong.

But I can't stop my feelings from taking over.

CHAPTER TWENTY-ONE

Vera

ONCE THE TRUCK IS GONE FROM VIEW, I MOVE toward the fridge and open it. There aren't many vegetables in the drawer, but I can make do with what he has. I search the rest of the cabinets and find ingredients for soup.

The moment he walked out of the door, I decided I would do something for him. Logan has been alone for so long, the same as I have, and I'd like to show him how this could work.

Even though our physical relationship is teetering on edge, I know we can find an emotional connection. I believe we already did, now I just need him to see it. I set out all the ingredients before I grab a pot and set it on the stove.

When I turn to the counter, I glance at the corner of the living room where Logan's laptop sits, along with my backpack. Quickly, I race to the bag and unzip it, finding my iPad and laptop. I pull out the smaller device and turn it on. If I can let my father know I'm safe, then I can relax.

Once the browser opens, I click on my mail link and open the inbox. I type out a quick message and smile when I imagine him reading it. I miss my father. He was a good man, nothing like Herbert.

I shut down everything once the message has sent and head back into the kitchen to start the soup. If Logan had a cell phone, I could've told him to bring some bread.

I smile at the thought of trying this, being in a relationship. It's not the normal way people meet, but then again, there are dating apps with success stories. I guess ours started out differently when we met all those years ago.

I think back on that day, reminding myself how big he looked then. Like a mountain of a boy, and he was only eighteen. Now that he's a man, he's larger than life.

I get to work on the vegetables and get them to simmering before I hear the truck again. I go to the door, pulling it open to find Logan coming up the steps. He reaches the porch before noticing me.

"Hey," he says, and I notice his gaze is no longer troubled. Perhaps the space has given him some time to think and come to terms with whatever this is.

"Hey." Stepping aside, I let him in and notice the two large brown paper bags he's carrying. Once we're shut inside, I follow him into the kitchen.

"What are you making?" he questions as he looks at me with an amused expression.

"Soup, you had some veggies that have seen better days, and I figured we could have it for lunch." I don't want to seem over eager, but I can't stop the flurry of butterflies that awaken in my belly when he smiles. I've not ever seen him grin like that, and I have to be honest; it's breathtaking.

"Okay, then." He chuckles. "Guess it's a good thing I got some freshly baked bread rolls." He starts unpacking the groceries and I help to put items in the fridge. We move in comfortable silence.

By the time everything is in its rightful place, we stop, both standing in the middle of the small kitchen. Our gazes locked on each other.

"This definitely will take some getting used to," Logan finally says.

"What?"

He takes a step toward me, closing the distance between us. "Having a beauty in my home, having her make me lunch, give me kisses when I want it."

"And all you had to do was kidnap me," I tease before leaning up on my tiptoes to press a kiss to his mouth. The beard he's been growing tickles my chin, and Logan's hands trail down to my ass as he lifts me against him.

My legs easily wrap around his waist, and my arms lace around his neck. Our lips mold together, his tongue darts out, dancing with mine as he deepens the kiss. Heat pools between my legs. A whimper of pleasure escapes me when Logan bites down on my lower lip, tugging the flesh until a sting of pain shoots through me, all the way to my clit.

"Logan," I mewl his name, and he swallows it with a kiss. He sets me on the kitchen counter before his hands roam my thighs, his one hand snaking between us as he teases the apex between my legs. "Logan." Another whimper tumbles free as he continues to play with me, pressing, circling, taunting.

"Come for me, Beauty," Logan coaxes me, his expert touch sending me spiraling into pleasure as I cry out his name again and again. Gently, ever so slowly, I come down from my high. The moment I open my eyes again, I look at him, meeting his dark gaze.

"Why…? What…?

"I just wanted to see you come," he tells me before leaving me on the counter and heading to the cooker to make sure the soup hasn't burned to a crisp.

I hop down to my feet and go to him. Circling my arms around his waist, I lay my head against his back, feeling his warmth.

"I like you," I tell him suddenly. The admission is true, and easy. It's not the other L word, but perhaps one day, it could be.

"I like you too, Vera," he responds, turning in my hold and wrapping me in his arms. "I like you too." His words sink through the strangeness of our situation, they tumble straight to my heart and settle there for later.

When I come downstairs for dinner, I find Logan at the counter. It's been set for two, with wine glasses and plates. My earlier lunch has been forgotten, and after spending the afternoon reading in bed, I'm starving. The scent of a grill hits my nose and I smile at him when he turns to me.

"It's nothing fancy," he says. Logan sets the plates on the counter. Both have a rather large grilled steak, mushrooms, and potatoes that look like they have melted butter drenched over them.

"Wow, this is amazing." I inhale the fragrances, and my mouth waters at the anticipation of having dinner with him.

"Being alone here, I've never had to cook for anyone. I hope it's okay," he tells me almost shyly. This is new to both of us. I've spent my life alone. I think we have so much more in common than he even realizes.

I pick up my cutlery and cut into the potato, which steams as I bring it to my lips. I blow a short breath on it, cooling it down before I pop it into my mouth. The flavor of herbs and butter mingles on my tongue causing me to moan in pleasure.

"Vera," Logan growls. I open my eyes to find him staring at me with those dark eyes and bore right to my very soul. "Keep that up, and I'll bend you over this counter."

"What about dinner?" I question playfully earning myself a chuckle. The sound is so foreign coming from him, but it's equally as charming. He may look scary from the outside, but I have a feeling that Logan's just a warm, affectionate teddy bear deep down.

"Eat," he orders while he uncorks the wine and fills my glass. The red liquid sloshes around as he pours. He picks up his glass, and I follow suit. "To something strange."

"To something new." My words hit me right in the chest. I look at Logan, and his expression isn't anger or frustration, he seems calm. Almost happy, if I have to gauge a reaction. "Tell me about you."

"What do you want to know?"

"The normal first date things," I say with a shrug. "Favorite food, color, song, you know." I continue eating, ignoring the way he's staring at me because I feel the heat of his eyes on me.

"I didn't realize this was a date." Logan sits straight, setting his knife and fork on the plate as he regards me. The corner of his mouth ticks up, and a smile graces his usually serious expression.

"Well, from what I gather, when a man cooks dinner for a woman, it's considered a date. And vice versa. And on dates, normally they get acquainted."

"Ah, I didn't realize that was the protocol. Well, Ms. Conreid, my favorite food is most definitely steak, the color would be the shade of green of your eyes, and song, well that has to be something hard and loud, maybe some Metallica." He offers me wink before he picks up his cutlery and continues eating.

"That was pretty romantic, Mr. *I don't do*

romance," I tell him, attempting a deep, gravely tone with the last few words. And I find myself laughing along with Logan as we settle into a comfortable conversation.

CHAPTER TWENTY-TWO
Logan

THE COUCH IS COMFORTABLE WITH VERA sitting beside me. We've spent the past hour chatting about our favorite things, what we'd like to do with our lives career-wise, and now that dinner is over, I want nothing more than to take her upstairs.

But I know what will happen. I'll lose control.

"Are you thinking about sex?" Vera asks, suddenly causing me to snap my gaze to her. "I only asked because I am." Her admission calms my erratic heartbeat.

"Yeah, I was actually."

"Can we try?"

My body says yes, but my mind and heart

say no. I want her, I do, but the *way* I want her would only end up with pain. I know it will. Even if I try to be gentle, to do things *normally* somehow, I know, I'll lose control.

"Logan," she pleads, moving over, so she's straddling me. "I want you to feel good too. You gave me so much earlier, I have never experienced pleasure like that. Let me show you how good it can feel."

Her wide eyes lock on mine, her mouth pouts playfully, and I can't imagine anything other than feeding her my cock. She grinds on me slow and steady, earning her a growl of frustrated pleasure.

A giggle escapes her lips before she slides off me and heads to the door. Without warning, she opens it and races out onto the patio. I'm on my feet in seconds, but Vera is fast.

She runs into the dark, leaving me calling after her. I can't focus, but I head out anyway, running toward the sound of her footfalls. I follow her, listening for more sounds as to where she's going.

"Vera!" I call her, but all I get in return is a giggle that drifts over the trees, and I'm left in the darkness. I stop, stilling all movement as I listen, trying to tune my hearing into the forest where my girl has now decided it's best to go running out into the night.

A few seconds later, I hear a crack of a branch and follow it. I know she can hear me, and I know she's hiding somewhere in these tall trunks.

"Vera, if you don't come out now, I'm going to whip you with my fucking belt, I swear to God." My voice booms, bouncing against the trees. But even as I attempt to find her in the darkness, my cock is hard, it's ready for her. Because the moment I find her, I'm going to give her a lashing, and then I'm going to impale her on my dick until all she can feel is me.

Another giggle, some rustling, and then I'm following her slight frame as it weaves amongst the trees. It's as if she's toying with my inner monster that's hungry for her. I want to devour her cunt, her tits, I want to make her scream so loud.

I turn around and slam into her tiny body, forcing her to the floor of the forest. I'm on her in a second, pinning her with my much larger frame.

"Is this what you fucking wanted?" I growl, my hands gripping her arms so hard, I know I'm leaving bruises, but I'm lost to the pleasure of the scene. She whimpers and mewls as she tries to fight me off, but I'm bigger, and stronger.

"Please, Logan."

Her plea means nothing to me as I reach between us to find her panties soaked. She's wearing barely anything, and on the cold ground, I'm sure she's freezing, but I can't bring myself to stop. My fingers dip into her cunt, pushing two in as I finger fuck her hard and fast.

My cock presses against her, and I grind myself against the smooth flesh of her thigh. I know she can feel me because her eyes go wide. Her legs are still wiggling under me, and it only serves to make my cock harder.

My other hand finds her throat. My mind goes blank, and pleasure takes over as I squeeze the sides of her neck, staling her breath which only earns me more whimpers of pleasure.

Her cunt drips onto my hand as I make her take my fingers. Again, and again. I feel her pulse, her arousal coating both digits, and I'm tempted to see if she'll accept them in her ass, but if I move, she'll fight back and run.

"This is what makes your pretty cunt wet?" I question in a low growl. "You wanted me like this? A fucking monster?" My fingers move faster as her hips rise up to meet my violent thrusts.

"Oh god," she croaks when I give her a short breath before squeezing again until I see her eyes roll back from my ministrations and lack of air.

The control I have over her is like a drug, and I need more of it. My body rocks against her as I feel her pussy tightening around my fingers and I hold her down, pinning her just like she asked me to and that's when I feel her shudder.

She cries out through croaked words as she squirts all over my hand and arm. Her eyes close, but her lashes flutter as I release her neck and see her look up at me.

"Fuck," she whispers in the dark when she finally comes back to me. "I've never..." Her words trickle into the night, and I want to nod, to agree with her, but I can't because I haven't allowed myself to find pleasure.

Silently, I move off her, standing as I offer her a hand, but she shakes her head. Suddenly, hands are tugging at my sweats and boxers as she takes me in her hand.

"Vera, no," I tell her. "It's okay. I'm—" My words are cut short when she wraps her pouty lips around my shaft, and in the dark, I close my eyes and bask in the need racing through my veins.

She works hard, taking me into her throat until I feel it pulse around my tip. My body is rigid, my veins spark and sizzle as pure and feral lust burns me from the inside out.

I bite down on my lower lip as a grunt escapes me. Her hand cups my balls, massaging and rubbing them gently. But then she squeezes as she takes me just that inch deeper into her throat, and I feel myself seize as my mind blanks out.

"I-I'm…" I can't get the words out as I feel my orgasm erupt violently, but Vera swallows every drop of me.

When I finally open my eyes, I look down to see her still on her knees, her tongue lapping at me as if I'm her favorite fucking candy.

"Get the fuck up," I bite out as anger takes over the desire. "Why the fuck would you do that? Do you know I could've hurt you?"

"I… I know, I just needed it." The innocence in her tone stills me. I'm losing my fucking mind, and I don't know how to be with her. Tonight was perfect, but right now, I feel like the monster that I'm convinced I am.

"Go get cleaned up." My order is clear. I can't be near her, or I'll lose my shit at her stupidity. No. She's not stupid. I'm the fucking idiot who should've not lost all my fucking control.

"Logan, I'm sorry. But—"

"Vera, I care about you, please just go inside. Sleep in my bed, I'll be up soon." Even as I tell her that, I know it's a lie because I'm raging inside. She nods and silently turns to make her way back to the house. Thankfully, it's not far.

I watch her disappear before I lean against the tree and look up at the sky. Even though the leaves cover most of the stars, I can make out a few twinkling here and there.

My chest aches. My whole body fucking aches. I've never been so lost in pleasure before. I have never in my life been so rabid to have a woman.

I don't know if she's good for me, even if she craves what I give her. I lift my hand to my nose and inhale her. The scent of her arousal is still intoxicating as it coats my hand, and I close my eyes and grip my cock.

I just had an orgasm, but just the fragrance of her juices makes my dick throb. I slowly stroke myself, picturing her beautiful face as she finds her release. My fist tightens, pulsing around my shaft as I emulate her cunt. The heat of her pussy took me in, sucking me deep, and I imagine my cock feeling those slick walls.

It doesn't take long, another two strokes, and I come hard, shooting my release onto the dark ground. My breathing is hard, short, and I have to focus to attempt at calming my heartbeat which is thudding painfully against my ribs.

"Fuck, Vera, what are you doing to me?" The question is lost in the darkness, and I shove myself back into my pants before I head to the house. When I reach the door, everything is silent, the lights upstairs are out, and Vera is nowhere to be seen.

I should go up to her, but I don't. Instead,

I go the kitchen and open the closet, which houses the cleaning materials. I find the bottle I'm searching for. Grabbing a glass, I pour a mouthful before swallowing it back quickly.

The burn of the bourbon is welcome. It's been years since I opened this bottle, but tonight, I am sure I could finish it without hassle. I pour another shot and swallow it quickly.

Taking the bottle and my glass, I head out onto the porch and settle on the wooden bench that sits in the one corner. It's not comfortable, but right now, it's going to have to do. I can't be in the same room as her.

I'm not even angry at her, I'm more rage-filled at myself. My feelings, emotions are taking over where Vera is concerned. It's not been that long since we actually spoke face to face, but I know her better than she knows herself. I know her body as if it were my own.

Do I really want to bring her into my life?

I'm sure if I went up there right now, she'd forgive me for what happened. I wouldn't blame her if she didn't, but with Vera, I realize that she sees past the volatile exterior to see the person I *want* to be.

And deep down, if I had to be brutally honest with myself, I want to be *that* man for her. I do want this to work. I want nothing more than to give her the house, the dog, and even a family.

I suppose a new day will come, and we'll find out if we can move past my insecurities. The darkness engulfs me as I look out at the trees that are now black. The night has taken hold of the cabin and as I sip the bourbon that I had kept stashed away, I feel like I'm at war with myself.

I should never have allowed her to talk me into sex. Or even just trying to be intimate. The last time we did this, she passed out. Granted, it was only for a minute or so, but it was still something I can never forgive myself for. This time, the hunt and chase had been erotic. It sparked something inside me that I had hidden away in the darkest depths. I want her. All of her, and I didn't think about the consequences.

I know I can't leave Vera, but her being here will ensure she's safe. If I had to take her into the city with me, she'd only be walking around with a target on her back. And that's not something I'm prepared to let happen.

CHAPTER TWENTY-THREE
Vera

I'VE LOST ALL SENSE OF TIME AND DAY SINCE arriving at the cabin, but it's been good. After Logan allowed me out of my bedroom, we've spent each day talking, getting to know each other on a personal level rather than sexually.

The sun hasn't risen yet, but I've been awake for hours. Or what feels like hours. Logan isn't in bed, and when I woke up, I reached for him, which is something I never expected myself to do.

I wonder if he's still feeling guilty about what happened because he hasn't really made a move to be intimate again. He shouldn't, and I wish he'd listen to me when I tell him so. But the stubbornness so clear in his eyes whenever he looks at me will always be a problem.

The door opens. My heart catapults into my throat, and I take him in. He doesn't say anything for a long while, so I move, pushing off the bed and padding over to where he's standing rigid.

"Good morning?" I ask because I'm not sure if it's good or not.

"I need to go away for a little while," he tells me without responding to my question. "I'm going to trust that you're not going to leave. My father found your apartment, and I doubt he's going to give up because you weren't there."

"Where are you going?" I look up at him. His eyes are dark, almost black from whatever is bothering him.

"I need to meet him face-to-face because this can't continue." His voice is husky as he takes a step closer to me. "I need some space from you as well. To think."

"What's there to think about? Why would you go to him? Won't he hurt you? He's dangerous, Logan." The words tumble free from my lips. The fear of what could happen to him if he ever came into contact with Herbert again sends cold dread through my veins.

"He can't hurt me," Logan tells me. He reaches up, cupping my face in one of his large hands. His touch turns the cold to warmth, and I no longer feel fear, but desire. His thumb swipes across my lips, and in the next second, he crashes his mouth to mine. His tongue sweeps against mine. We twist and tangle, tasting each other. The coffee flavor from him makes me smile against his mouth.

Finally, Logan pulls away. "I wanted to walk away, to send you away," he admits, lacing his fingers through mine. "But I can't do that."

"Why?" I ask, looking up into the darkest eyes I've ever seen. He no longer seems guarded around me, which is good, but there's still a hint of restraint that he's holding onto.

"Because I'm a selfish bastard," he tells me. A small smile tilting his lips upward. "And I can't imagine you walking away from me." He motions toward the door. "Freshen up, I'll be in the kitchen." He gives me one more kiss before he leaves, making his way down the stairs. "Come down when you're done."

Once he's disappeared, I head to the bathroom and shut the door behind me. I use the toilet before I step in front of the basin. It's small, a one-person sink, where I open the tap and splash my face with the icy water.

My reflection is blurry for a moment. Grabbing a towel, I dry my face and take a long look at myself. My eyes are bright, shining with . . . I don't know . . . happiness? He said he can't let me go, which means last night's events haven't pushed him over the edge, but I need to know why he's trusting me alone in the cabin. Completely alone.

I freshen up, using my toothbrush and toothpaste before I head out of the bathroom and toward the steps. The clanking of dishes comes from the kitchen, and I wonder if he's making breakfast.

Tentatively, I take a few steps and come face-to-face with Logan. He's not wearing a shirt. The taut muscles of his torso tense when I finally reach the bottom and make my way toward him.

He sets a plate in front of me piled high with pancakes, as well as a mug of coffee. He doesn't say a word but turns away to finish whatever he's busy with at the stove. I pick up the fork he set out and cut into the soft, fluffy goodness. The moment I bite into the pancake, my taste buds burst with the sugary syrup that's been trickled over the stack.

"This is good," I tell him through a mouthful of my breakfast.

"I don't normally cook as you know by now," he responds before spinning on his heel, and setting another bowl down, which I notice is filled with scrambled eggs. "We don't have anything else in the house, but I'll make a store run before I leave."

"Why do you have to go?" I ask again, looking up at him.

He leans back against the counter, his dark eyes piercing me. I watch as he folds his arms across his chest, making his muscles bulge. He's huge. He could easily pick me up with one arm.

"I need to see him. To finish this."

"What if—?"

"Nothing is going to happen to me," he assures me, but I don't believe him. I know his father; the man is a monster. Logan may believe he's a bad man, that he's not worthy of happiness, but I've known Herbert all my life. The man is nothing short of the fucking devil.

"I'm not saying it will." I stop eating, setting the fork down. "I'm scared, Logan."

He nods solemnly, and I know what he's about to say. "You should be."

"Not of you. You're nothing like him," I affirm what I've been thinking all night and morning. "You're a good man." He chuckles at me, but I shake my head, pushing off the chair and making my way to where he's standing. "You're nothing like him. I want this," I tell him. "I want you."

I place my hands on his folded arms, the touch tender, but his body goes rigid as if I'm about to strike him. The heat between us is palpable. His gaze burns through me, reminding me of last night, of what we did.

"I want you to do it again."

"That was a mistake. Last night's events will never happen again. As much as I want you," he tells me, his voice turning dark. "I can't have you."

"But you just—"

"Us, together, it's dangerous. I'm a danger to you, Vera, and I can't hurt you. Did you not see what happened? I fucking hurt you!" The boom of his voice bounces off the walls. I half expect the windows to shatter, but they don't.

"It was the first time we tried it, that you tried doing that. I'm okay." I smile, but I know it's no use. He's never going to believe me.

Logan unfolds his arms. His fingertips tentatively stroke the column of my neck, and he whispers, "You're bruised. I've marked you, and I'm so fucking sorry."

"Do you want me to hate you?" I ask, causing the movement of his fingers to stall. His gaze flits to mine, locking on me for a long while. "Do you?" I want him to say no, to tell me that it will all be okay, but I have a feeling he won't.

"I want you to run away, to escape the darkness that I live with. You deserve better. You should have a family, a beautiful home, a man who loves you. Not someone who can hurt you."

The crack in his voice is the only evidence that he's hurting. The expression on his face is stoic, and I wonder if he's spent the morning practicing what he's going to tell me. Perhaps the way he schools his features is his way of showing the pain that's so clearly bothering him.

"No."

"Vera," he murmurs my name. "I'm not the man who can give you the life you deserve."

My chest aches, tightening painfully as his confession engulfs me. "You don't have a say in what I want or need," I tell him.

"You can't fix me!" He shoves me backward, stalking by me. I watch him grab his keys and wallet before tugging the door open. "Don't leave this cabin, or I will find you and bind you to the fucking bed." The door slams closed, causing me to jump in shock at the anger so clearly emanating from Logan.

Once I'm alone, I sit on the chair, shock still coursing through my veins. The roar of the truck dissipates the farther away he gets, and soon, all I'm left with is silence.

CHAPTER TWENTY-FOUR
Logan

I'VE FUCKING LOST IT.

I should never have lost my cool, but Vera does something to me that scares the shit out of me. She makes me feel things I have no right feeling. Emotions I buried a long time ago come to the surface when she touches me, when she looks at me like I'm her hero. I'm far from it.

If she can only admit that I'm bad for her, then she can move on. I know now that no matter what I do, she's always going to see me as a savior. I can't be that. I'm not some prince coming to save the princess, I'm nothing like those damn fairytale heroes.

I've spent my life trying to get over the fact that I will never have a family. I can't spend my life with a woman when all I want is to watch her sleep, to use her limp, lifeless body for my pleasure. *How can I ever give Vera that and ask her to accept it?*

When I pull into the lot of the diner, I contemplate going inside. I want to sit down, have a beer, but I know nothing will calm me down now. I need to consider what I'm going to do. Letting her go is the one option I'm convinced about, but then again, she *wants* this.

Can I be selfish and keep her for myself?

No. This is the one time in my life where I need to think about someone other than myself. She doesn't need my father or me. She should have a normal life. The moment I think it, I recall where we met—online. The website in question was designed for predators to find their prey. And I know she's only going to go back there to seek what she needs.

I can understand that because I crave it too. It's not an emotion you can tamp down. It's so much more. It's visceral. Sighing, I lean my head back against the seat and look up at the roof of the vehicle. I focus on nothing in particular but the thought of keeping her.

I sit in the truck for a long while, watching couples from town walk in for the lunch rush. There are a few singles who follow the path toward the entrance, but I don't join them. Instead, I'm lost in thought about that night.

"Shit, Vera," I call to her. Her body is limp, but her heart is thrumming. She's warm. Her lashes slowly flutter as if she's fighting the fatigue. When she finally looks at me, I breathe a sigh of relief. "I fucked up. I'm so sorry."

It feels like I've apologized to her more times than I can count in the past few days. I should never have put my hands on her, but she felt so good, so . . . normal. My body reacted to her. It's never done that while I've been with anyone else.

She curls her body into mine as if she's afraid I'm going to leave. Her delicate fingers twist in the material of my shirt, and I allow her to hold me. I can't find it in myself to touch her, not again.

I've only ever hurt those I love. All my life, I've taken beauty and marred it with my darkness, with the desires I can't control. At first, I denied it. I thought it was all a joke, but the more I craved it, the more I realized I truly am a monster disguised as a man.

Vera coughs, and my body goes rigid. "Don't leave me," she pleads into the material of my shirt, tugging me impossibly closer. I can't move. Instead, I lie still, waiting for her to release me once her breathing evens out. But even when she finally falls asleep, she doesn't let go.

Her hold on me is tighter than expected. And my heart thuds against my ribs. The muscle I long since forgot about is awake and wanting to leap into her small hands. It's been so long since I've given myself to another person having Vera inadvertently need *me is strange.*

Silence greets me in the dark. Vera's soft breaths warm me, and I close my eyes for a moment to revel in her nearness. I know she's not mine to keep. After tonight, I know I can't trust myself around her, so for now, I allow myself to enjoy her body curled against mine.

Briefly, I consider the idea of her healing my brokenness. Or just fitting her shattered pieces alongside mine. But I can't risk hurting her again. As much as I crave her, as much as I want to own her, seeing her eyes close and her body turn lifeless makes my mind race with reasons I should let her go.

I'm so fucked up.

I'm cursed, and there's nothing that can change that.

Even though Vera wants to try, I don't think I could ever bring myself to allow her near me in that way again. Time passes, but I don't go home. I can't. The ghost of her touch still burns my skin.

My phone buzzes wildly on the seat beside me. Picking it up, I notice Dax's name glaring at me from the lit-up screen. I swipe my finger to answer and press the device to my ear.

"What's up, man?"

"He knows where you are. We've tracked him down to a forest. It's—"

I don't listen to the rest of his explanation as I twist the key to start the engine. I'm tearing through the streets, trying to get back to the cabin. My heart is thumping like a drumbeat against my ribs, causing my chest to tighten as fear twists in my gut.

My phone buzzes again, but I ignore it. My focus is on getting to Vera. If she's in danger . . . No, scrap that. I know she's in fucking danger because my father wouldn't just walk away and allow her to live her life. She ran from him, and I know he's going to do something to her. Something far worse than I could imagine.

CHAPTER TWENTY-FIVE
Vera

The cabin is so silent I can't focus on anything other than my senses pricking, trying to hear if I can make out a rumble of an engine coming this way. But I have a feeling Logan won't be back for a while. When he walked out, I knew I'd taken it a step too far.

Instead of pushing him, I should've waited. I saw the guilt in his expression. Last night was something else. Poignant. My body reacted to my orgasm so powerfully I lost consciousness, and with the tightening of his hand on my throat, I let go. I felt safe for the first time in years. I wish he understood that.

Logan may think he's dangerous, that he's someone I need to stay away from, but there's a part of him that also believes I'm made for him. I need to make him see that I am not afraid. It's taken me years to come to terms with these *needs,* and I don't want him to think I'm a fragile girl.

I'm all grown up, and I know what I want. I think I've always known that Logan was mine. Even when I was younger, remembering his face, his eyes, the way he looked down at me when I was so enamored with this boy in a suit who looked like he should grace the pages of a magazine.

The older I got, the more I realized that even though he walked away from me, my heart would find his again. Fairy tales aren't always filled with rainbows and happily-ever-afters. They're also drenched in darkness, curses, and bad guys. I've learned over time that fiction imitates real life far too often, or perhaps it's the other way around.

I grab another mug, filling it with steaming coffee before I settle at the counter to read the newspaper from a few days ago. Logan left it out, and I soak up all the information I can. I really should be rummaging around in the cabinets, or even trying to find a way to escape. But I'm not longer here as a prisoner, I'm here because I want to be with him. So, I sit and wait for him to return.

I have to be honest with myself. I don't want to go back to my old life. Right now, I know I can't because Logan has changed me in ways I can't explain. I would never be the girl from the small apartment in the little town of Pine Lake again. And I certainly am not the girl who walked out of Chicago, leaving her father to serve his life sentence in prison.

But I am still the girl who's afraid of Herbert Oakridge because he's the only person who can hurt me. If he ever finds out where I am, I doubt I'll be alive to see the next sunrise.

Sighing, I move to the couch, crossing my legs on the cushions and sipping the still-warm coffee. The bitter taste bursts on my tongue, and I savor the heat coming from the cup. It's not winter, not even close, but I feel a chill as if a storm is about to hit. Being out in the wilderness is strange when I'm used to being around people.

The door flies open, crashing against the

back wall as it bounces on its hinges. I shoot off the couch, only to come face-to-face with the man who practically bought me from my father. Logan hasn't returned from wherever he went, and now I'm standing facing the man I ran from, the one I hid away from for years.

"I thought I'd never see you again," Herbert says in his cold, rage-filled tone as he saunters inside. Two men, both dressed in black suits, white button-up shirts, follow him into the cabin. It doesn't take him long to reach me. I can't move because I'm stuck between him and the couch. He steps closer, and I fall back onto the cushions.

"I . . . I didn't mean—"

"You know," he says, interrupting my mumbling, "I thought you'd be a good girl for me." His words send poison trickling through my veins. "But you're nothing like that, are you?" His dark brow arches as he questions me. "Tell me something, Vera," he continues. His dark eyes look so much like his sons it's scary. "Do you like playing house with my son?"

"I never wanted to marry you. I—I told my father that. I—I was just trying to live my life,"

I tell him, but my voice breaks on the last word. I inwardly curse myself for the fear lacing my words.

"With my son? He deserted you!" His voice bounces off the wall, the threat hanging on every word. "He walked away from his chance, and your father agreed that you would be mine."

"I'm not a possession you can push around, bartering me." I push off the couch, needing space from this man I know is going to hurt me. There's no doubt about it; he isn't someone who can be reasoned with. I've known him all my life, and I know for a fact that even my father was afraid of him.

I pray inwardly that Logan will return, but with the two bodyguards standing at the door, and his father right up in my face, I have a feeling he won't make it in time. And even if he did, they would be armed, and the thought of Logan getting hurt because of me sends cold dread racing through my body.

"You," he sneers, grabbing my hair, tugging me backward until I fall against his large, looming frame. "Are mine." There's no longer a question that he's angry. My throat feels thick, and my lungs work hard to pull in a much-needed breath. "And I'm here to show my son that he may try to save you, but he's no fucking hero."

Herbert pushes me onto the floor. The pain that shoots through my arm as I fall against the wood of the coffee table causes me to cry out in agony.

"Perhaps my son likes the helpless ones." Another dark chuckle follows me as the two men who were behind Herbert are now in front of me. One of them has a syringe in his hand. The clear liquid filling the device makes my chest tighten in fear.

"What is that?"

"Something to show Logan he's not some fucking hero who can save his damsel in distress," Herbert tells me, which only kicks up the level of fear that's captured me.

Confusion settles around me as the men drag me up the stairs. I watch as Herbert follows, and my legs kick out in an attempt to shove him down to the floor, but he's too far out of reach. My arms flail as the large hands grip my biceps, and they pull me into the bedroom where Logan had me captive.

"What are you doing? Please, please don't hurt me," I beg, looking directly at Herbert Oakridge, but from the expression on his face, I know pleading for mercy isn't going to make him change his mind.

He moves toward me as both bodyguards hold me down on the mattress. My legs kick up and out, but I don't make contact. Herbert's hand raises, and I notice the syringe. He leans in and offers me a sickening grin.

"Time to go to sleep, Vera," he chuckles darkly. The sound is low, animalistic. He doesn't sound human. The sharp needle pierces my skin, and I watch as he pushes the plastic bit down, injecting me.

"No! What is that? No!" My voice is scratchy, my throat dry and painful as the words are ripped from me. I feel the heaviness in my limbs, my eyelids fighting to stay open, and as I look at the man who's finally gotten what he wants, I can no longer fight.

Darkness overwhelms me, and weariness takes hold.

"Please," I mumble, sounding like a voice

from a dying radio. "Please don't." The last thing I remember is a shot ringing out before I'm stolen from the light and thrown into darkness.

CHAPTER TWENTY-SIX
Logan

ONE OF THE MEN GOES DOWN, AND THE OTHER spins on his heel, startled at the way his friend fell to the ground. He lifts his hands in surrender, but I don't feel like showing mercy as my finger presses the trigger. Another bullet empties from my gun, hitting him right between the eyes. Looks like target practice paid off.

It's only when I reach the middle of the staircase that I see him. My father stares at me long and hard. Disappointment and disapproval shine in his dark eyes. The only difference between now and my younger years when that look would hurt me is I no longer give a shit about him.

"What the fuck did you do to her?" My

voice is low, menacing, as I move closer to him. But Herbert Oakridge doesn't cower in front of me. No. His son, now a man who no longer answers to him, doesn't scare him because he knows his life is over.

"I thought I'd see how long you both can last if you're given the type of woman you like," he smirks, the corner of his mouth lifting in satisfaction. My gaze darts to Vera. She's not moving. Her hands are clasped across her chest. She looks so peaceful as if nothing can hurt her.

"What. Did. You. Do. To. Her?" I ask again, turning my attention back to my father.

His expression doesn't help the rage coursing through me. I want to shoot him, to see how well he does with a bullet straight through the heart, but I can't do anything until I know how to fix her.

"You'll know soon enough, son," he tells me easily. The tension in my shoulders tightens. "If you put down that gun, I'll give you my terms."

"Terms? This isn't some fucking game," I bite out, my finger still poised on the trigger. I want nothing more than to pull it, to show him I'm in charge, but I don't because I'm not sure what he's done to Vera. The asshole knows I won't do shit to put her in harm's way, and that only angers me more.

A loud bang from downstairs captures my attention. I want to move, I know I should, but instead, I stay focused on my father. He doesn't seem at all perturbed by the fact that I have a gun pointed at him.

Seconds pass before I speak again. "You have your team of assholes coming in here to kill me?"

"I don't want to kill you, son," he tells me as he settles in the armchair overlooking Vera's sleeping form. "I want to prove to you that you're just like me, son. She'll never accept you for who you are." He gestures with his chin, pointing at the beauty in a deep slumber. I want to go to her to make sure she's still alive, but I can't move because I feel cold metal against the back of my head.

"Then why is there a man pointing a weapon at me?" I challenge him, needing to know the truth. "Because from where I'm standing, his finger can slip, and I won't be in your way anymore."

"Why are you so convinced I'd like you dead?"

"Because I took her, I hid her away, and you want her for yourself. You signed the agreement, forcing her father, your longtime friend, to give his only daughter to you." My voice is chilled, ice dripping from every word, because I can't believe the man who I'm looking at is even related to me. Yes, we may share similar features, but the evil so clear in his dark eyes has nothing on me.

He smiles, the action slow, intentional, because nothing my father does hasn't been thought through. That's what he taught me all those years ago. You must be calculated if you want to make your enemies fear you.

I watch his movements, his one leg crossing over the other. He steeples his fingers under his chin, and he regards me with cool aloofness that makes him seem almost mechanical. That's who my father is, an uncaring monster. The more I look at him, the more I realize I'm nothing like him.

Vera was right. I may be slightly broken, but I am not an evil monster like the man who raised me. "Tell me," I say finally. I've had enough games. It's time to walk out, kill all the men he's brought into my home, or be killed. The latter doesn't sound like an option to me, because the moment I take my last breath, he'll claim Vera. And that's the last thing I want or need.

"I want to prove to you that you're no good for her," he tells me easily. "You're so far gone you don't see it. I chose to take her as mine because I knew that you'd never be able to give her the life she should have."

"Neither can you." My frustration is clear in my voice. "Does mother even know you're here, trying to lay claim to a girl young enough to be your daughter?" Venom drips from my words, and I notice the slight flinch on his face. He doesn't give away much, but I know I've just hit a nerve.

"Your mother is traveling. She's enjoying her life," he tells me, and I wonder if that's code for him having her killed. There's dark satisfaction in his eyes as he watches me. "Come inside, Logan." He gestures with his hand for me to enter the bedroom. I don't want to move, but with the metal weapon pointed at my head,

I take two steps, and I'm at the foot of the bed.

"What do you want here if you're not taking Vera?" I ask him, still holding onto my gun. I could shoot him, but then his men behind me will pull the trigger, and I'll be on the ground with Vera exposed to them. And that's not a chance I can take.

"I want you to see yourself through their eyes," he chuckles, nudging his chin toward the bed where my girl is lying still.

"What is wrong with her?"

"Have you heard of an induced coma?" Dad arches a brow at me, the corner of his mouth tipped upward, and I nod. "Well, our little beauty is sleeping soundly for a while. She'll awaken in a few days. I made sure to give her a good dose of the drugs needed for this little experiment."

"You're sick," I bite out, making my way toward him, but the moment I take a step, the click of the gun trained on me has me halting my steps. My father rises, shrugs, and then makes his way past me toward the door. "Where the fuck are you going?"

"Oh, I'm going to watch this from the security

of my own home." The grin on his face makes my body shudder with rage and revulsion. "I can see this will be very entertaining." He turns and shuts the door, and that's when I hear it. They're trapping us inside. Something is being shoved against the door after the lock clicks. "My men will stay behind to ensure you don't leave. Unless you'd like to jump out the window," he tells me through the wood.

I raise my gun, cocking it before I pull the trigger. A chuckle resonates through the barrier, and I realize I missed. Cursing inwardly, I set the gun down on the vanity before turning to Vera.

"Nice try, son," Herbert mutters. "But you're way off. Goodbye," he tells me before I hear his footsteps going down to the ground floor. I'll give them an hour before I break out of this fucking room and kill the men I know are in my house. My father's plan will not work because I'll never hurt my beauty.

My attention is on my girl as I take her hand and press a kiss to her knuckles. She's warm, her cheeks flushed, and her lips pursed. I don't think she will ever forgive me for this. I left her alone when I should've kept her close.

"I'm so fucking sorry," I tell her sleeping form. "I should never have left you alone. This is all my fault, but I promise you, I'll make it right."

I don't know how I'm going to do it, but I'll make sure her life is safe once more. The thought of killing my father is still at the forefront of my mind. I want nothing more than to see him fall for his devious plans.

I pull my phone out of my pocket and scroll down to Dax's name. Hitting call, I press the device to my ear and attempt to focus on how the fuck I can get out of here.

"Hey, what's going on?"

"I need you to send a team of men to the cabin," I tell him. "Herbert Oakridge thinks he can fuck me over, but it's time I take the asshole out."

"He's your father."

"I don't give a shit, Dax. He's taken it too far." I know my best friend won't deny me. He knows how lethal my father can be. "He has two of his men in the cabin. I'm locked in a room with Vera. He's drugged her. She's in an induced coma."

"What?" The surprise is evident in his voice. My father's done some questionable things before, but this is taking it just a step too far outside of my comfort zone. I grew up around illegal acts, I heard things that would most probably get him arrested, but when he came into my home, threatened the woman I love, he made a mistake.

"I need your help."

Dax answers me quickly. "There's no question about it. You know I'm going to be there for you no matter what." I breathe a sigh of relief. "I'll have a team out to you in the next few hours. Give them time to arrive, and don't do anything stupid."

"Me? Stupid? Since when?" I try to make light of the situation, but it's no use because I'm livid. I could easily rip them apart.

"I'm serious, Logan. They know you're strong, Herbert is no fucking idiot. He'll have planned for you to try to break out of there," Dax warns, and even though I know he's right, I don't think I can sit around and wait.

"Get them here as soon as possible," I tell

him before hanging up and moving toward the window. There aren't any cars outside, just my truck, which is parked near the front door. Other than that, I suppose the men must have been left here without a way to leave. Perhaps I can get them to side with me. My father may pay their salaries, but I can offer them freedom from his organization before they get hauled into cells beside him.

With a slow twist, I unlatch the window with the small key I kept in my pocket, pushing open the upper half of the pane. The cool breeze fills my lungs the moment the wooden beams snap open. In an attempt to see the lower floor, I lean over the bottom half of the window and notice one of the men, dressed all in black, outside smoking a cigarette. That means there's only one of them inside.

I turn toward the door. Moving silently, I twist the handle but find it locked. I don't have the spare keys on me, which only sends frustration coursing through my veins. I should've kept the fucking batch of keys when I left.

I pick up the gun, realizing there's only

one way to do this—with brute force. Aiming at the doorknob, I pull the trigger twice. The resounding clank of metal bounces around the small bedroom.

"He's trying to break out!" The shout goes off just like I knew it would. With a grin on my lips, I step back, waiting for the assholes to make their way inside. Because the moment they do, I'll kill them both and get my girl out of here.

CHAPTER TWENTY-SEVEN
Logan

I LISTEN TO THEM, PULLING AWAY WHATEVER they've barricaded the door with. I'm ready, my hand poised, my finger on the trigger, waiting, breathing deeply. My chest aches with worry and fear, and I want nothing more than to get Vera out of here. Since my father knows where we are, it won't be long until he gets a team of men out here to keep us imprisoned.

The door flies open, the hinges squealing at the sudden movement, and my finger presses down on the trigger. The shot rings in my ears as I take down the first asshole. The second man stops, falls to the ground, and moves behind the wall, which is solid. I can't take a shot until he's moved into view.

"If you come out, I'll spare you. But if you come near her, I'll make you pay," I tell him, not moving from my spot where I'm sheltering Vera if he does decide to shoot from around the corner.

"He's going to find you, and when he does, this will all be the biggest mistake of your life," the asshole grunts. His voice is low as if he's trying to whisper the threat at me, but I don't give a shit what my father does to me.

"And the biggest mistake of your life will be when I end you," I inform him as I move closer to the doorway. I tread lightly, making sure to not alert him that I'm almost at the threshold. The gun still held out in front of me.

The moment I'm close enough, I spot his leg and take aim. My finger presses down, and within seconds, I've hit him right in the shin. A groan of agony bounces off the walls of the hallway, and the clank of his gun falling to the floor has me moving forward.

By the time I've moved both bodies outside

and deep into the forest, covering up the shallow graves, I hear a car pull up to the house. I don't have to look to know it is Dax's men. When I turn around, I find my old friend Kael along with Axel. Both men I've met a few times since knowing Dax. Even though we weren't necessarily friends, they were always around with Kael's sister, Theia. She was the one who hung around to catch Dax's attention.

"Seems like you got this all sorted," Kael smirks, offering me a hand to shake. I'm reminded of the times we used to watch him spend hours at the easel while we drank beers. The long, curly brown hair with the ripped jeans and T-shirt suit him. He looks like he's really relaxed after what went down with his dad.

"I managed to get two clean shots in. I need to clean up inside and get Vera somewhere safe," I tell him.

"Well, Axe and I can help with that. I have two cars circling the area, making sure there aren't any more assholes hiding away," he tells me.

"Thanks for coming." I slap him on the shoulder before I turn my attention to Axel. "It's been a while, man."

"It's been far too fucking long," Axel responds, his British accent thick. "Dax mentioned you're coming back to the city with us?"

"Yeah." I nod. "I need to end this shit storm my father started. Going after me is one thing, but he went after my girl." Both men nod in understanding. They know what it's like to have the women in their lives in danger because of some asshole who should never have intervened.

"Sounds good," Kael says before following me toward the cabin. There's not much inside I need to pack, merely some clothes for Vera and myself, and my computer, along with her devices I grabbed from the apartment when I took her.

Anything else can be locked up. Even if Dad gets into the house, he won't find anything he can use against me. I'll have the most important thing—Vera.

"Do you want anything to drink? Or are you ready to head out?" I ask as we step into the living area. The open plan offers up a view of the kitchen as well.

"I'm good. I think the sooner we leave, the better." This comes from Axel, and I know he's right. "If you want to shower first, we'll wait." He gestures to my clothes, and I notice the blood and caked-on mud I've brought in from burying my father's men.

"Yeah, make yourselves at home." I leave them downstairs, making my way up to the bathroom, where I quickly strip off and hop into the shower. I can't be long. The more time we waste out here, the easier it will be for Herbert to send men back to claim Vera.

Back in the bedroom, I pull out my phone and tap out a message to Dax to ask him to send a doctor to my apartment once we get there. I want Vera checked out. I don't trust my father. Even if he says she'll be okay soon, I'd rather have a medical professional take a look and assure me she's alright.

By the time we reach my old apartment, I'm exhausted. We got Vera into the bedroom, placed her on the bed, and I've finally gotten an hour's worth of sleep. The moment Axel and Kael left, I flopped on the sofa and allowed my eyes to shut. It's been one whole day, and she's still not awake.

I know the doctor will be here soon enough, but I'm stressed. My muscles are stiff, and my jaw is aching from me grinding my teeth. Tension has taken hold of me, and I know it's not going to let go until she's awake.

I've been scrolling through websites, looking up information on what my father did to her. What I found has my blood boiling. She could be out for a couple of days or even weeks. The need to go to him is at the forefront of my mind, but I'm not leaving here until I know my Beauty will be okay.

The buzzer sounds and I push to my feet to answer the intercom. "Yeah?"

"Doctor Novak here for Logan Oakridge," the man answers, and I give him instructions on how to get to the apartment. When the elevator dings, I open the door and meet the older man. "Nice to meet you. Dax said your girlfriend needed a check-up?"

I nod. "To be honest, I don't know what's wrong with her. I think she's been put into an induced coma," I tell him as I lead him into the apartment and toward the bedroom. "I just need to know she's safe. That she'll wake up soon."

He doesn't respond. Instead, he just follows me into the bedroom. At Vera's side, he opens his bag and pulls out a stethoscope, along with a small flashlight. I step back, allowing him to do his thing, but my eyes never leave the bed.

Time ticks by, and with every passing second, my stomach tightens with anxiety. Finally, after I'm not sure how long, the doctor looks at me.

"She'll be fine. She is in a sort of dreamlike sleep, but she'll wake up soon. I can't tell how long exactly. It depends on her fighting through whatever drug was administered."

I sigh in relief, shaking the older man's hand before saying, "Thank you, doc." He packs up, and I escort him to the door, shutting it behind him.

Once Dr. Novak leaves, I pick up my cell phone and dial Dax's number. He's at the club right now, but I know he'll answer, no matter what. Seconds into the ringing, his voice comes over the line.

"Hey, man," he greets. "Sorry I couldn't

come through. I had shit to deal with at the club. Are you okay?"

"Yeah, just looking forward to meeting my father face-to-face."

"When are you making a move?"

Shaking my head, I lean against the soft cushions of the couch. "Not for a while. I need to wait for Vera to wake up. If I leave her and he has his goons find her, I'll never forgive myself."

"I know what you mean. Let me know when you make your move because I'll be right beside you. Theia is capable of running the club without me for a while."

"I can't ask you—"

"You're not asking," Dax interrupts me. "I'm telling you I'll be there because we're friends. I consider you a brother, and I'm not letting you walk into that shithole alone. I know my men will be right behind me as well." He is confident in his promises, and I know he'll never let me down.

His assurance calms me somewhat. Even though I know I should refuse him; I don't. I know I can't ask them to walk into whatever my father has planned, but at this stage, I don't have a choice.

"Okay," I finally acquiesce. Something tells me if I did refute his offer, he'd be there anyway because that's the type of man Dax is. He's there for his friends, he doesn't hide from danger, and he's a violent motherfucker who will kill anyone who stands in his way.

"Good," he tells me. "I better get back to work, but if you need anything at all, you have my number." He hangs up without a goodbye, and I lean my head back against the couch once more. My eyes focus on the ceiling. The smooth, white paint has no marks, no scuffs, and I stare at it until I feel weariness taking over me.

CHAPTER TWENTY-EIGHT
Logan

A WHOLE TWO DAYS HAVE PASSED, AND VERA is still asleep. She's been flinching, but nothing more than that. Each time she does, my heart stutters. The chair I'm sitting in overlooks my bed, where my beauty lies sleeping.

Lying in bed beside her is difficult. Especially when she's asleep and looking so beautiful. All I want to do is touch her, to feel her body against mine. I lean in, pressing my lips to hers. My eyes close, and I revel in her warmth.

My father was right in one respect. I want her, even like this. My mind is filled with images of all the things I can do to her while she's like this. We're alone, we're safe . . . for now . . . and I want to let go and lose all control. But I could hurt her, and that's not an option.

I take in her sleeping frame, her hands crossed over her chest, and her lips slightly parted. Her body is so still. I can't stop myself from placing my hand on her leg, feeling her warmth. I trail my fingertips up her thigh, toward her hip, and over her flat stomach. She's soft, delicate, like a doll that is also fragile.

My cock is rock-solid against my jeans as I watch her lashes flutter along the apples of her cheeks. I wish for a moment this was a fairy tale, and my kiss could wake her because all I can think about right in this moment is fucking her senseless.

My phone buzzes, dragging me away from her and my dark thoughts. My father's number glares at me from the bright screen. I don't want to answer it, but I force myself to swipe my thumb along the screen.

"Haven't you done enough?" I bite out angrily.

"Have you fallen to your natural cravings yet, son?" he chuckles into the speaker, causing my fingers to tighten around the device, squeezing it. I want nothing more than to end him, to wrap my hands around his neck and watch him struggle for breath. "Because you know you will. You want to do it. Don't you?"

"Fuck you!"

"I thought so," he tells me noncommittally as if I were falling right into his trap, and I must admit, I think I am as well. My gaze casts over to Vera, who looks like a vision with the silver light of the moon streaming through the window.

"I'm not a monster," I inform my father, but deep down, I don't believe it. He's right. I close my eyes and focus on my breathing rather than how my blood is running hot in my veins, how the desire is taking over me, and how much I do want to fall prey to the need so clearly gripping me.

"You know, when I was your age, I went through something very similar," he speaks, slow and steady as if he's waiting on my shocked response. But I don't give it to him. "Your mother stood by me. She knew I had no control over what I craved so deeply. It's inside your DNA, Logan."

"I will never be like you."

"You already are." His voice drips with

satisfaction. "Look at her, son. Really take her in, so helpless. Her body is yours, a toy to revel in while she sleeps. That's what you are, an Oakridge. It's in our blood to crave darkness."

I fist my free hand, the nails digging into the fleshy palm. Pain skitters up my arm, but as much as I fight it, as much as I want to deny it, my father is right. It is in my veins, and I don't know how to get it out.

"The more you fight it, the more violent it gets." Those are the last words he speaks to me before he hangs up, leaving me in the darkness with Vera. While she sleeps, I battle with myself, and it's a war I'm slowly losing with every minute that passes.

What if he's right about the violence?

What if I can't stop myself and hurt her?

"No," I tell myself. "I'm not him. I'll never be him." I turn away from Vera, my gaze locked on the window, taking in the city below. It's been so long since I stepped foot in Chicago it looks foreign to me. The lights glitter in the darkness, and from so high up, the cars look like toys, racing from point A to point B.

My hand instinctively moves to my cock,

the hardness still straining the front of my jeans. I glance over my shoulder, looking once more at the girl I've fallen for. I knew I loved her before, but this is something more. It's become all-consuming.

My feet move on their own accord. I'm at the bed in seconds, leaning over her, looking directly at the way her chest rises and falls. How her breasts look mouthwatering. The yearning that courses through me has my body shaking.

"I want you, so fucking much," I tell her. The silence that responds is ear-piercing. It's wrong. So fucking wrong, but I can't stop my hand from moving to her lips. I swipe my finger over the plump bottom one.

Moving over Vera, I hover along her body, my cock aching and throbbing against the apex of her thighs. It would be so easy just to feel her, to press myself against her, harder and faster. But I don't. I focus on my mouth molding over hers. A soft whimper tumbles from her when I kiss her.

My eyes snap open, taking her in. She's still asleep, she's not moving, but when my tongue darts along her lips, tasting her flavor, she moans once more. It's a soft, gentle sound, but I hear it.

Her fingers jolt, and the moment I'm convinced she's waking up, no more movements come. I wait for a long time, just watching her, but there are no more signs of her being aware of what's going on, of what I'm doing to her.

I lean in closer, listening to her breaths, and I whisper in her ear, "You don't know how difficult it is for me not to fuck you right now." I trail my hand down her body, remembering the day she role-played for me, lying on my bed, pretending to be asleep. When I felt her body limp, as she tried to feed the hungry beast that resides within me. She gave me that. Something no other woman has ever given me.

"I love you." My words are a whisper, skittering along the smooth, creamy flesh of her cheek. "I've fallen in love with my Sleeping Beauty, and I don't know if I can ever let you go. My inner demons want so much to play with yours," I tell her. "They want to devour you just like this."

A soft murmur tumbles freely from her parted lips. "Please." It's barely audible, and for a moment, I am convinced I imagined it.

Perhaps the drugs are wearing off. Maybe she can hear me. My hand moves between us, and I press two fingers against her pussy. Her heat is scorching. The shorts she's wearing are tight against her mound, and I circle her clit through the material.

Her body jolts at the contact, but I don't stop. I can't. Another moan slips free from her, and I continue my ministrations until I feel her wetness seeping through the clothing. My fingers would be drenched if I slipped my hand into her panties, but instead of doing that, I focus on her.

The soft tremble that shoots through her suddenly causes me to still all movement. She's silent, but her hands are shaking, her lashes are fluttering wildly, and I can see movement behind her eyelids.

I push on, teasing her pussy until I see the corner of her mouth tilting. Her lashes dance along her cheeks, which are now turning a soft pinkish shade. My cock is fighting its way through my jeans, the zipper almost painfully pressing against the shaft.

"Oh god," Vera whimpers suddenly as her

eyes flick open, and they lock on mine. Her body shaking with the orgasm, I've just coaxed from her. "Logan?"

"My Sleeping Beauty," I mumble down at her. "I'm sorry. I shouldn't—"

"I . . . That was amazing," she whispers, her hands coming up to cup my face. The gentle touch sending me spiraling into darkness. "Where are we?" she questions, realizing the walls are no longer wooden logs, and the light shimmering through the window is slightly different from being out in the middle of the forest.

"My father found us, found you," I tell her, not moving. Needing her closeness to focus on my confession. "He drugged you. You've been in an induced coma for three days."

"What?" Her mouth falls open in shock. "Where are we?"

"In Chicago," I inform her. "I'm here to take the asshole down. What he did to you was taking my feud with him too far." I reach for her face, trailing my knuckles along her cheek. The softness forcing the monster back into hiding. "I'll never let him near you again."

"I trust you," Vera whispers.

"You shouldn't."

"You could've hurt me, but you didn't. You could've done so much worse," she murmurs, looking directly into my eyes as the guilt slowly seeps its way through my veins.

"He was right."

"Who?"

"My father," I tell her. "He told me I'm broken. That I'm a monster, and he was right. I couldn't resist the pull of your beautiful sleeping body. I craved to touch it, to use it for my pleasure." My voice cracks on the last words. Pain is evident in them, and I know Vera heard it because she's shaking her head.

She may try to disagree, but I know it's true.

I am a monster.

I'm certainly not the prince she needs.

I'm the dragon she needs to slay.

CHAPTER TWENTY-NINE
Vera

He won't believe me. I know he won't. I can see the resolution in his eyes. Being so torn and broken is something I can understand. But he can't push me away because we are made for each other. I'm convinced of it.

"I want you to do something for me," I tell him, keeping my voice steady. I push off the bed and make my way through the apartment. Finding my way into the bathroom, I don't bother stopping to take in the beauty of my surroundings. I'm on a mission, and it's something I need to do before I know Logan will believe me.

I read something online about Logan's ffliction. A while ago, while searching for ways to find pleasure in my desires, I stumbled upon a website that spoke of kinks that most people balk at. It's where I found my solace, knowing I wasn't alone.

I open cabinets, shutting them again when I don't find what I want or need. Logan's fierce demeanor shrouds the space when he stops at the door, his face a picture of confusion and worry.

"What are you doing, Vera?"

"Looking for something," I tell him without glancing at the man I know will have a fit if he knows what my plan is. On the website I'd found so long ago, I read about a man and his wife who were in our *predicament*.

The wife wanted to role-play a scene of force. The man, on the other hand, enjoyed her asleep, and they found a way to get both. Logan isn't cursed or broken, he's merely a man who enjoys somnophilia, and I don't balk at something like that. I never judge others for their wants and needs, the same way I hope he doesn't when he hears my proposal.

I don't know how I knew he'd have them, but when I hit the final drawer, tugging it open,

I find the bottle I need. I pull it out, lifting it so he can see what I have, but before I have time to make my case, he's shaking his head.

"No."

"Yes."

He turns and heads down the hallway into the bedroom with me hot on his heels. He's on the bed, his head in his hands as he tugs at his dark hair. I can feel the frustration flowing from him.

"Please, just hear me out," I beg as I drop to my knees in front of him. "Logan," I call to him, my voice dripping with a plea. When he finally lifts his gaze to mine, I settle on the bed beside him. "Let's try this. I want to try this."

"Why? I'm a fuck up, Vera. This is a fucking joke," he grits through clenched teeth. I watch his angular jaw tick with frustration. I want so badly to help him, to hold him and tell him it's all going to be okay, but I know he won't believe me. He needs to allow this to happen before he believes it.

"You're not a fuck up, and I'm not going anywhere," I tell him.

Logan shoots to his feet and begins pacing

the carpet. "My father was right when he said I'm just like him. I want this, Vera. I crave to take you while you're just there, lying in bed oblivious to what's going on. I want to feel your warm, limp body tremble as I slide into you. I can't think of anything else."

His admission should scare me, but it doesn't. All I want is for him to finally find himself with me. I want him to try this, to give it a chance, because if he doesn't, I know he'll do the one thing he's been thinking about—push me away.

My chest tightens when I think about it. When I consider walking away from him, my lungs struggle to pull in air, and my heart clenches so painfully I can't fathom my life. Perhaps it's stupid to think I can fix him, and maybe, in all honesty, I don't want to.

"I want that," I tell him honestly. I pray he can see the admission in my eyes. I wait for him to look at me, and when he does, I keep my gaze locked on his. The need for him to see my truth is running rampant through me. "Don't let him win, Logan. Your father was trying to get in your head. You're nothing like him."

"I need time." He turns, heading for the door, but before he leaves, he glances at me from over his shoulder. "Don't leave the apartment. You're staying inside safely until I get back. I need to clear my head." And then he's gone, leaving me with the bottle of melatonin. I've had these before. A sleep aid, and when my doctor advised these were better than getting something that would be addictive, I always kept a bottle in my medicine cabinet. One or two when I couldn't sleep always helped, but this time, it's different. This isn't insomnia I'm fighting—it's the man I've fallen for.

Pushing off the bed, I head into the rest of the apartment to explore. The furnishings are beautiful, classic, yet modern and tasteful at the same time. It's nothing like my small apartment, but it feels like home, nonetheless.

Three closed doors are waiting for me down the hall. The first one is the bathroom. The second one, which opens when I twist the handle, is an office. The desk is dark wood, with a large black leather chair behind it.

I notice a laptop sitting on the desk, which I quickly make my way to. If I can log into my email, perhaps I can find out how my father is doing. It's been months since I was allowed to call him, since he told the guards he didn't want any communication. Sadly, I let it be when I should've fought his choice.

When I lift the lid of the computer, I find it opens to a password screen, which has me cursing out loud. *What could his password be?*

I sit for a moment, thinking back on the time I've known Logan. The only thing I can think it could possibly be is his screen name—Broken Prince—which I try, and it easily logs me into his computer.

Breathing a sigh of relief, I open the browser and get to work logging into my mail account and getting a message to my father. If he knows I'm back in the city, perhaps he can call off Herbert and that stupid contract he signed.

I want to be with Logan, and I know he wants me too. He just needs time to come to terms with his wants and needs. I can't help but smile because I'm the younger of us two, and it seems I've accepted my desires before Logan could ever fathom what his were.

Society forces us to hide who we are. If

you're not a sheep following the herd, you're shunned, and that causes people to tamp down the feelings that come naturally to them. Shaming someone for a kink, as long as it's legal, is something that's always bothered me.

And now I have to wait until Logan accepts who he really is.

And he also needs to come to terms with the fact that even though he may not be *normal* in the eyes of society, I love him.

And I'm not leaving him.

CHAPTER THIRTY
Logan

THE ROOM IS ICY COLD, THE FIRE NO LONGER dancing in the darkness. I watch him for a long while before I move closer. My father, the man I grew up equally fearing and looking up to, is no longer the same person. He's become a monster, demented and dangerous.

"So, you really think happiness is in the cards for you and the little beauty?" he questions as I train the gun on him. The barrel aimed at his forehead. One shot would kill him. The bullet would hit him right between the eyes.

"I told you, I'm nothing like you," I tell him.

"If you shoot me, you'll be just like me," he assures me confidently. There's a hint of pride in his voice, which angers me so much more than it should. "When you take me out, you'll be the new Oakridge the men answer to. With that kind of title, you need to be focused on the end game."

"What's that? Stealing from the poor so you can have the royal title of King?" The sneer on my face has him chuckling as he shakes his head in amusement. I've always been obedient, giving in to whatever he wanted. His orders were law, but that's changed.

He regards me for a while before he says, "You don't get it. Do you, son? I didn't do this for me." He moves around the desk, settling behind it before opening the top drawer and pulling out a folder. "It's your destiny to be with her," he explains.

I snatch the manila folder when he holds it out to me and flip it open. My eyes scan the wording, noting it's the contract he had Vera's father sign. With every sentence I read, my body stills, and my heart leaps wildly against my ribs, banging a beat that steals my breath.

"This . . ." My words fail me as I try to make sense of what it says. "This can't be true. How would you even know I would find her?" I look up, taking note of my father's satisfied smirk. "How. Did. You. Know?"

"As a father, I learn how to ensure my son gets what he needs. I've known for a long time you'd find your way to her, and she'd find her way to you. It was planned, all of it." He doesn't move, waiting for me to respond. I'm not sure how. Him making sure I found Vera, that she would even want me after everything that happened, wasn't something he could've known would pan out.

"This is a joke, right? I mean, there would be every probability it wouldn't work. What would you do then?" I look at him, taking in his expression. The asshole is so overconfident he doesn't even realize this could've gone badly.

"You underestimate my influence on your life, Logan." He settles back, steepling his fingers under his chin as if he were a goddamned king. And at times, he likes to think he is, but no more.

I'm done.

"Your games end here," I tell him, shoving the folder across the smooth, varnished desktop. "Vera is not yours. She is free of any contract you have with her father."

"No, she's not mine, but like the contract states," he speaks, chuckling while he pauses for effect, "her firstborn will be taken and raised by the rightful owner of the organization. You will not raise that child, and you and your sleeping beauty will forfeit your heir. That is, if you stay with her. If you decide otherwise, perhaps I can rethink my terms."

"That's bullshit!" My voice booms in the large room, the echo of it bouncing off the walls as my rage takes over. I circle the desk, my hands on the arms of his chair as I lean in to meet my father's glare dead-on. "Nothing I have, nothing that Vera and I build together, will be yours. Do you understand me, old man?"

"What *you* don't understand is that I can find you. Anywhere you run or hide, I will hunt you down, and I will take what is rightfully mine." His sneer is ever-present, but I chuckle loudly at his statement. What he doesn't know is I will take him down, but I don't tell him that. Not yet. Once Dax has the information I need, I'll be delivering my father straight to the authorities. And then he will spend his life in prison.

"Stay out of my life. Stay away from Vera.

And never contact me again," I tell him, playing his game, ensuring he thinks I'm oblivious. I turn and head for the door, stopping short before I glance over my shoulder at him. "And if you do decide to act out your childish games, I'll come for you, and I won't stop until I watch you take your final breath."

The moment I'm free of the building, I take a deep breath and tap out a message to Dax, letting him know about the encounter. His response is what I want. "We'll get the sonofabitch." Nodding to myself, I make my way to the truck and hop into the driver's seat. Time to go back to Vera and talk her out of her stupid plan of sleeping pills and sex.

Even as I weave through the streets, the idea takes hold of me, and by the time I'm pulling up to the apartment block, I'm hard. My cock aching for her, and I wonder if I can try to show her pleasure and find my own release just like a normal man.

Pushing my way through the doors, I step into the waiting elevator and hit the button for the top floor. With every passing number, I wonder what she's been up to. I have a feeling

Vera's been snooping, but I know there's nothing I want to hide from her. Even if she's gotten into my computer, there aren't any secrets between us, not anymore.

After I open the apartment door and step inside, I shut myself in and call out, "Vera?" but get no response in return. "Beauty?" I call to her again, but still, she doesn't reply. My feet move quickly as panic sets in, and thoughts of my father doing something to her while I was in his office makes me race up the steps toward the bedroom.

None of the other doors are open, and when I step into the bedroom, I find her on the bed, her body wrapped between the sheets, her back bare to my gaze as the material covers her pert ass.

She's naked.

She's asleep.

And my zipper gets even tighter.

"Vera?" I whisper as I move toward the bed. When I reach the mattress, I find a note on the pillow beside her. Picking it up, I scan her neat, scrawled handwriting.

My Broken Prince,

I want to try this. I want you, inside me. Even if I'm not completely lucid. I love you, Logan, and I trust you, no matter what.

Your Sleeping Beauty

"You bad fucking girl," I mumble to myself while shaking my head. I cannot believe she did what I told her not to do. Thankfully, she didn't leave the goddamned apartment. Setting the note on the nightstand, I go to her, tugging at the soft sheet, and it falls away, gifting me a view of her smooth, curvy body.

Her ass is pert, the cheeks calling to me to touch her. Spine sneaking from her neck down to her beautiful behind. I want to lick my way from bottom to top. Her thighs are slightly splayed, one knee bent at a ninety-degree angle, offering me a glimpse of her smooth pussy.

Her long, dark hair is fanned across the pillow, her pouty lips slightly parted as she breathes deeply. She's completely and utterly at my mercy, and my cock happily throbs against the material of my jeans, wanting a taste of her tight, sweet cunt.

This is pure torture.

I shouldn't do it.

But I know nothing can stop me now.

CHAPTER THIRTY-ONE
Logan

Tugging at my T-shirt, I pull it up over my head. My hands move quickly, unbuttoning my jeans and pushing them down my thighs. Keeping my boxer briefs on, I scoot onto the bed behind Vera.

She's warm and soft. I trail my fingers over her shoulder, reveling in the tiny goosebumps that rise on her skin. A small whimper falls from her lips as I make my way over her breast, taunting the nipple between my thumb and forefinger. I twist it, tugging until it hardens into a peak. My mouth waters to taste her, but I refrain for now. Instead, I move my hand to the other nipple, finding it pebbled, and I offer it the same attention as the first.

Her body is perfect. Even with small, silver stretch marks in places, and the gentle nips of what I can only assume are scars from childhood, she still is utter perfection. I lower myself toward her thighs, tugging her gently until she's on her back, her legs splayed, offering me a view of her smooth, yet perfectly trimmed cunt.

The mound has a dark patch of hair, but the lips of her pussy are smooth, and I can't stop my thumbs from tenderly touching them, feeling her warmth. I open her to my gaze, taking in the slightly wet, glistening pink of her entrance.

I lean in, my nose inches from her as I take a long, deep inhale. Her scent is like a drug shot right into the vein. The high is like nothing I've ever experienced.

No noise comes from her mouth, but when I make contact with her pussy, my tongue lashing the smoothness, a gentle mewl tumbles from her, and I continue my ravaging of her tight, beautiful cunt.

With every lap of her, I feel her wetness coating my tongue. I can't stop, my eyes shut tight as I focus on her, only her. I don't think about anything outside this moment of contact.

My tongue darts into her, tasting the sweetness, and I'm lost, a man in the middle of an ocean, and all I want is her as my savior.

Her body trembles and I can't help but enjoy the way she's responsive, but not coherent. The darkness clouds my mind as I think about taking her right now. Shaking my head, I taunt her with my index finger, teasing her entrance as I slide one digit into her tight pussy. The gentle pulses of her cunt feel like heaven when I slide in and out gently.

"You're so beautiful, Vera," I tell her as I finger-fuck her while licking at her wetness that coats my tongue. The flavor bursting on my taste buds. My body aching, my cock so hard, so painfully rigid, I can't focus on anything other than the need to come.

Once her body has responded, her cunt wet and needy, I pull my finger out and kneel between her thighs. Her body limp and lifeless, waiting for me. I can't stop myself from pushing down my boxers and taking my cock in hand. The silky-smooth flesh hard, engorged with desire for her. I fist myself before tapping the crown of my dick on her clit a few times, earning myself another gentle mewl from my sleeping beauty.

The wetness of her slicks my cock, and I position myself at her entrance. The tight pussy wrapping around my shaft perfectly. She was made for me. Her body accepting my slight nudging as my hips move forward, driving my dick inch by slow and torturous inch into her.

Soft, dick-jolting murmurs come from Vera as she takes me. Her body engulfing my cock as I slide into her wet heat. The pleasure that zips down my spine is inexplicable, and I must close my eyes, biting down on my tongue to keep from coming too soon. She feels too good. Too fucking perfect.

Vera's body shakes, her thighs tremble, and I watch her lips part on soft breaths and mewls. Her lashes flutter on her cheeks, dancing gently, and I wonder if she can hear me.

"You're a bad girl for doing this," I tell her softly. I inch inside her, deeper, feeling her warmth envelop me as I finally sink balls-deep into her body. The feeling of her wetness is too much to bear as I look down at her slumbering body.

I reach down, teasing her nipples as I pull out and slide back in. I make love to her as if she were fragile, as the tsunami of guilt and desire twirl together. I want her more than anything, yet I'm only here because she's asleep. The need that burns inside me has turned me into a monster, yet my girl still loves me.

"How can you love a monster?" I question her, knowing full well she can't tell me. I continue my ministrations on her nipples, suckling one into my mouth while twisting and tweaking the other. My cock fucks into her pretty cunt, enjoying the pleasure that's sparking every nerve in my body.

I feel alive.

I feel like a man.

But still I know I'm a monster.

"Logan," Vera mumbles my name, and I realize she's waking. I still all movement, my gaze snapping to hers. My mouth still latched on her hardened bud. "Please." Her moan is fuel to the fire raging inside me. I'm fighting a war, and it always felt like I was doing it alone, but I'm not because Vera is here.

"You're a bad girl," I tell her as my hips

move back, and I slam inside her harder than before. The soft whoosh of breath tumbles from her mouth, and I swallow it with a kiss. Her tongue sleepily dances with mine, and her lips tilt slightly into a small smile.

"Love you," she slurs the words, her hands twitching as she awakens from her slumber, and I'm even more turned on. I didn't think I would be, but the more she's becoming coherent, the more I crave to claim her.

"You're mine."

She attempts a nod. I continue moving, pulling out, thrusting my hips against hers, and soon enough, she's lifting herself to match my movements. We're made for each other, fitting like two torn scraps brought together and held there as if we were never meant to be apart.

Her cunt tightens, pulsing around my cock, and I realize now that she's awake, she's reaching her first climax. I move faster, deeper. I lift both her legs, her ankles draped over my shoulders as I piston into her.

More mewls, more dick-jolting moans, and a whimper of my name, over and over again, cause my body to go rigid as I fight off my impending orgasm. I need this to be good for her. She did it for me, and now I need to ensure she's found pleasure as well.

I watch her tits bounce with every thrust. I smile down when I see her lashes dance once more, and her eyes meet mine.

"I fucking love you," I admit to her, knowing she'll see the truth in my eyes. Her body pulses around my cock, and I am convinced it's my confession. "I love you, Vera. More than any-fucking-thing." Once more, her body responds by tightening, sucking my dick deeper, and my name falls from her lips.

And I know I'm a man obsessed.

CHAPTER THIRTY-TWO
Vera

My body aches, but the moment I open my eyes, I realize he's still inside me. The thickness of him stretching me. My mind is still fuzzy, but I feel the pleasure of him hitting *that* spot, and my toes curl.

"Fuck, Vera," Logan grunts. "I can't hold back for much longer." His voice drips with pleasure, with pure, unadulterated need. He moves slowly, his hips driving into mine at such a steady pace I'm certain he's trying to make this last longer.

"Please," I manage to whimper, and a feral growl rumbles in his throat. His body is taut, his arms rigid at my sides as he looks down at me. He's heavy, fucking me into the mattress, but I love it. Every second of his cock thrusting into me makes my body hum with pleasure. I didn't think it would be like this, that he'd be able to do this with me half awake, but he is.

"Fuck, your cunt is so tight, so warm and wet," he tells me through gritted teeth. "I've never experienced anything like this," he admits, and my heart soars. Emotion thickens in my throat, and I blink back the tears of happiness. I've given him something nobody else could.

"Fuck me, Logan," I plead, and he does. His body moves quickly. His cock sliding in and out with every thrust, as he hits my G-spot. The motion sends my body spiraling into the abyss of pleasure, and I grip the sheets with my fists. I tug at the material as my legs spread wider before my ankles lock behind his ass.

"Jesus, Vera, I'm going to come," he murmurs in a low grunt, and I nod, but I can't tell what's happening because Logan reaches between us and circles my clit, pressing down on the bundle of nerves before pinching it, causing me to cry out, and then I feel his warmth filling me. "Drench me, Vera. Give me all your sweet juices," Logan coaxes as he continues thrusting, and my body shakes as I feel the pulsing deep within me.

"Oh god," I cry out when he pinches my clit once more, and I come hard. My toes curl, my fingers find purchase on his shoulders, and my nails dig into the strong muscles as I claw at him. Every nerve-ending in my body is blazing—sparking and sizzling with pleasure. "Logan . . ." I murmur his name, but no other words come, and finally, he stops moving.

We lie there for a long while in the silence. Our breaths mingling, becoming one. He's warm, heavy, holding me down just like I imagined so many times before. The need for him to take me has finally come, and he gave me so much more.

"Please don't be angry," I plead while I look directly into his dark eyes. "I just needed you. And I didn't know any other way to do it. I craved you so much that—"

His mouth crashes on mine, stealing every other apology I was about to spew, and his tongue seeks entrance, which I give gladly. We kiss with an energy that makes me tremble beneath him. Logan hikes himself onto his elbows as he hovers over me. His lips mold to mine, our tongues dueling for dominance, but I submit, offering him me, all of me.

When he finally breaks away, his gaze penetrates me down to my very soul. "You shouldn't have done that without my permission."

"I'm a big girl, Logan," I tell him confidently. "I can do something if I feel I want to. And I needed you to see that I'm not fragile or broken. But most importantly, I had to make you see that this" — I gesture between us — "is not a bad thing. We are meant to be together. You fit with me, and I with you."

He looks at me as if he's still torn. For a moment, I think he's going to push away from me and tell me I need to leave, but then he nods. "I went to see my father," he admits before rolling over and pulling me into his arms. His warmth coats my thighs as if he's marked me inside and out. His strong, inked arms wrap around me, holding me hostage as he speaks. "He does have a contract with your father, but it's not what either of us thought."

"What do you mean?" I lift onto my elbow,

needing to look him in the eye. There's darkness in his expression, his brows pinch together, and his body is rigid. "Logan, tell me."

"I read the contract, went through every word, and he's laying claim to our first-born son if we have one. He said he knew we'd find each other again, and if we didn't, he would've captured you, kept you in the house until I returned."

"I don't understand."

"Neither do I. He is convinced that our son, will be the heir to the Oakridge fortunes. But what I don't understand is what he'll gain from it. Granted, my father doesn't love me, that much is clear, but what I don't get is why he wants *us* to have a son for him to claim."

"Maybe there's more to it?" I suggest, but the confusion painted on Logan's face is swimming around my mind as well. It doesn't make sense. *Why allow me to run away and let Logan leave if he wanted us together?* Surely, he could've just held us both in Chicago and pushed us into each other's paths.

"There is definitely more to it. But before I go snooping into my father's things, I need to get him out of the way. The problem is, once the cops take him in, they'll be the ones who have access to his documents before I even have time to get there."

"Then the only way is to get him out of the office with a ruse of some sort?" I consider this for a moment. "I could call him, wanting to meet to talk, and you could go in and see what you can find."

"No."

"Why?"

"I don't know what he's capable of, Vera. You're not going anywhere near him." Logan's tone is no-nonsense. And I know arguing with him won't help, but playing it safe will also not be an option. I push onto my knees, my naked body catching his attention for a moment before I speak.

"Logan, remember what I said. I'm a grown up, and if I choose to do something, then you really can't stop me unless you decide to bind me to your bed. If I meet him in a public place, I'll be safe."

His expression turns from anger to frustration at my words, but he knows I'm right.

If there's more to *our* story, I want to know what that is. It could be dangerous, but if we don't try, we won't know. And my father is still refusing to talk to me. After my email, I used Logan's phone and tried calling again, but they told me he is not taking any calls from family or friends.

"I don't like it, Vera."

"I know you don't, but right now, we don't have a choice." I move over Logan, straddling his waist. His big, strong hands grip my hips as I roll them back and forth. "I mean, if you could just try it my way, you'll find I'm right." My words are a mere whimper when I feel him harden under me.

He locks his gaze on mine, and a small smile dances on his lips, tilting them seductively as he regards me. "You're a seductress," he tells me. I continue grinding on his cock, feeling the heat of him pulsing against me.

I'm wet again, craving another feel of him filling me. "I want you right now." My admission causes his eyes to flutter closed, and a groan falls from his full lips. His body is rigid, his fingers digging into my hips, and I know he's focusing on the pleasure and not the fact that

I'm the one in control. I have a feeling Logan enjoys the control more than his obsession with me being asleep.

I slide against him, feeling the tip of his erection against my clit, which forces a whimper of pleasure from me. I do it again, and again. The heat of him mingled with the wetness of me is an erotic combination of desire and pleasure. I move forward and angle myself, causing him to slip inside my pussy.

The pained pleasure of his thickness stretching me steals my breath as I lower myself until he's fully seated. Every inch of his cock is inside me, and I'm trembling at the way he feels throbbing in my core.

"Fuck, Vera," Logan mumbles, his hands pulling me forward and pushing me back. Even with me on top of him, he still wants the control. He uses me for his pleasure, my body a device to keep the heat between us raging like an inferno.

He drops one hand to my pussy, his thumb circling my clit as I ride him. "Look at me, Logan. I want you to see me." My voice is raspy as I plead with him. He gifts me his dark gaze. He strums my clit with an expert touch as I rise and sink down. His other hand reaches for my neck, squeezing so tight, I gasp.

"Shit," Logan grunts when my pussy tightens around his cock. I feel it. He feels it. We're both close, reaching for the edge, the precipice of desire about to push us both over. "Come for me, Beauty, come hard." His growl is feral. My hips move faster, harder, and he sinks in impossibly deeper, hitting that spot that has stars bursting against my eyelids, and I croak out his name as my orgasm crashes over me.

Moments later, Logan fills me with his seed, and I realize, in that moment, I can never want another man to take me. I'm his Sleeping Beauty, and he's my Broken Prince.

CHAPTER THIRTY-THREE
Logan

Dax, Kael, and Axel are seated in the club when Vera and I enter. There's a girl on stage practicing her pole dancing, but none of the men are looking at her. I know they're all taken, and so am I, but I don't know how Dax runs this place with that going on every day. I guess having Theia, his submissive, around does distract him from the lure.

"Hey, man," Dax greets me, offering a hand, which I grab and shake. "And this is the beautiful Vera," he says, looking over to my girl.

"Hi, nice to meet you," she responds shyly. That's what I love about her. Even though she can sass me, her sweet, submissive nature comes through when she's beside me.

"Nice to meet you finally. Didn't realize this asshole was capable of love," Dax taunts, which earns him a punch in the shoulder from me. "Just stating facts." He ushers us to a table where Axel and Kael offer up a wave to Vera and me.

"So," I start as I settle into the chair. "I need to get this shit done and dusted. He has that contract that states her dad has signed over our first-born son, should we have one, to Herbert Oakridge. My father is a fucking monster."

"My men have looked it over. Don't worry about that. What we did find, which will help us, is a shit-ton of his communication to underground organizations. Embezzling money, but also trading in weapons to Russia and Germany. Not sure what else they can dig up if they go in deeper," Dax tells me. "We can take him down just with that information alone."

"I'll just walk into his office and kill the arsehole," Axel chuckles, leaning forward as he picks up his beer and swigs the cool liquid.

"It's not that easy. If anything were to happen to him, I would be the first in line to take over, as well as the first person they'd come to as a suspect."

"Why?" This comes from Kael, who's leaning back in his chair. He looks as relaxed as if he were on the beach.

"There's a clause in my father's will. If anything were to happen to him that wasn't natural causes, there must be an investigation. Me first, then my mother. We're both on the list as the first people to point fingers at."

"Fuck," Axel curses as he drinks his beer, his gaze trailing the club, but focusing back on me. "What about if we did it silently? Send him away on *vacation*," he says, the last word in air quotes. I like his suggestion, but it's not going to work. My father's clever. He'll have men watching every move we make.

"If it were that easy, I would've done it ages ago," I inform them. My phone rings before I have time to continue. I pull it out, finding my father's name glaring at me. I consider not answering but realize if he's up to something, perhaps I can drag it out of him. Pressing the device to my ear, I answer, "Nice to hear from you." Sarcasm drips from my tone.

"I'd like to set up a meeting. You, me, and Vera. We'll sort this out like a family."

"And what makes you think a family with you is what I want?" I challenge, poking the bear, which I know is a bad idea.

"My suggestion would be to come here and listen to me. If Vera would like to see her father again, you'll agree to my terms. I'm willing to work on this with you, Logan." The tone of his voice is so cold I can't help but shiver at the implication of him killing Vera's father, his best friend. Or at least former best friend.

"Fine. We'll be there." I hang up, my gaze taking in Vera, who's staring at me wide-eyed. "He wants to see us both. If I can get him to back down, it will give us time for Dax to get in touch with his contacts." Even though I'm connected, most of the men I know get paid by my father, and they'll never go against him.

"Are you sure you want to go in there?" Dax leans forward, his elbows on the table as he regards me. The man is big, as tall as I am, and just as broad shouldered. He looks strange, sitting at a table so small.

"I have to. If I don't, he'll come after Vera

again, and I can't let her get hurt."

Vera's soft voice breaks between us. "What if he does something to me while we're there?"

I glance at her before answering, "Then I'll take the fucker out in his own home." Pushing off the chair, Dax rises with me, offering his hand. I take it and shake, knowing he would be there if need be.

"You have my number," he reminds me with a small grin.

"I do. I'll call you when I know something. Keep digging," I tell him and offer my hand to Vera. She laces her delicate fingers with mine. "Kael, Axe, thanks for coming to help when I needed you," I tell the two guys. I've only met them a few times over the years, but they're good guys.

"Of course," Kael says as he shakes my hand.

Axe rises, tipping his fingers in a mock salute. "Anytime you need some fucker dealt with, you call me."

I turn and make my way out of the club with Vera hot on my heels. She's taking the atmosphere in. I can see her head darting left and right as she watches the girls strut around in their skimpy outfits.

"Do those guys have girlfriends?" she whispers under her breath when we reach the door. "I mean, they work in a place where girls are stripping."

"The ladies dance," I tell her. "They're professional. And yeah, all three have women." I chuckle as her eyes go wide. "Why? Don't think you can handle me working in a place like that, Beauty?"

"No. I mean, I trust you . . ." Her words taper off into the silence that surrounds us. She's shy, I can tell by the way she looks at the ground, and her cheeks are flushed.

"Listen to me, Beauty." I stop, cupping her face in my hands. "You're mine. No other woman would ever come close to being what you are to me. It's going to take us time to find our feet in this relationship, but I'm willing to try if you are. No woman has given me what you have, and I'm not about to allow that to leave my life. I'm not walking away from you, not this time."

Her face is a picture of affection and

happiness when she looks up at me. A quick nod and I press my lips to hers. "Let's go." Her words force me forward, and I know whatever we're about to walk into will change our lives forever.

Either I'm going to kill my father, or he's going to finally realize what an evil bastard he is and step back from everything. One thing is for sure—he isn't getting his claws into mine and Vera's lives or future family.

The drive through the city is silent, but the tension is heavy between us. The cab is filled with anxiety, which twists in my gut. Even though I won't allow anyone to hurt Vera, the thought of losing her grips my heart painfully.

By the time we pull up outside the house, I'm so tense my white-knuckle grip on the steering wheel feels as if my hands are glued it. I want to tell Vera to wait here, but my father made it understood he wanted to see us both.

"When we walk in there, you stay behind me." My order is clear. "Do you understand me, Vera?" I glance over at my girl in the passenger seat. "I don't want you hurt in any way, and if he tries anything, I couldn't live with myself if something happened to you."

My girl meets my stare, a small smile on her trembling lips. "I know. I'm not going anywhere without you." Her promise calms me somewhat, but it can't erase how something dark twists in my gut.

It feels as if it's the calm before the storm.

And I've always hated rain.

CHAPTER THIRTY-FOUR

Vera

LOGAN EXITS THE VEHICLE WITHOUT ANOTHER word. I watch him round the front before getting to my door. He opens it, helping me from the seat. Our fingers are laced as we make our way toward the massive front door.

Carvings adorn the dark wood, and I can't make out what they are before the portal slides open, and a beautiful woman smiles at us. She steps aside, allowing us entrance.

"Mr. Oakridge is in the office," she tells Logan, but when she glances at me, her face pales in shock. "You look just like the lady." She says, her mouth falls open, but she doesn't say anything more.

"What lady?" I ask, but she only shakes her

head and scurries away.

It's strange, but when I look at Logan, I notice he seems as confused as I am. I follow him as he leads me through the entrance hall that reminds me of my childhood home.

I grew up with a beautiful, middle-class house. My father was always there for me. My mother died when I was young, and I don't remember her much. Daddy always told me I was just like her with my beauty, but strangely enough, he never kept photos of her out like I would imagine any other widower would. There was only one I found when I was fifteen. When I saw her, I recognized her immediately—a dark-haired beauty who stole my father's heart.

We reach a door I'm guessing is Herbert Oakridge's office. Logan doesn't knock; he pushes it open and steps inside with me following a step behind. He doesn't allow me to come into view, so I don't know why he stops short.

Silence hangs heavily with something I can't quite pinpoint.

"What the fuck is this?" Logan questions as he moves farther into the room. I finally take everything in, and I notice it's not only Herbert in the room. There's a woman with her back to us. Slowly, she turns on her high, spiked heel, and I can't help but notice how perfectly poised she is. Dark hair spills from the clip holding her hair up.

She's dressed in a dark pantsuit with bright-red Jimmy Choos. She's elegant. But when my gaze lifts to her face, my heart leaps into my throat, threatening to choke me. My lungs struggle for breath when she's fully facing me.

"Mom?" My shock is clear in the way I mutter the word. I believed my mother was dead. All my life, I recall the pain my father lived with. I remember how he would tell me I looked just like her, that he could look at me and see her beauty. The heartbreak of him losing her was so evident in his demeanor; I promised myself never to love someone so much. But as my hand tightens in Logan's, I know I've broken that vow ten times over.

"For a long time, I thought you'd be the good girl your father told me you were," she says, her voice cold, pure ice. "But the moment you ran after learning you'd have to live in the

Oakridge household, I knew I'd failed you. Perhaps I shouldn't have left." Her shrug is nonchalant as if she's talking about running to the store to grab some bread and milk.

"How are you . . .? I mean . . ."

She meets my gaze, and I see it. I'm the younger version of her. I wonder how my father even looked at me knowing his wife was a fucking liar.

"The only thing I wanted since I was old enough to understand how this world we live in works was the Oakridge name. But Herbert had already found his wife, the love of his life," she sneers, anger dripping from the words. "And I had to marry your father because that was what was expected of me."

"Why? Could you not have refused?"

"Darling," she laughs coldly, shaking her head as if I were a child who needed to be spoken to like I'm not fully functioning. "When you grow up with a family who respects tradition more than anything, with a father who hungers for goddamned power and money, you learn to respect it too."

"So, you married Dad because you felt you

had to?" I ask her. "Because you couldn't stand up for yourself as I did?"

"You stood up for nothing," she spits as rage burns in her gaze like an inferno tearing down everything in its path. "You ran away when things got hard. Dad told you a lie, but I ensured that even though you run, you'll still bear an Oakridge."

"Yes, *I* will, not you," I grit out, stepping closer to her. "I will marry Logan, and I will have his baby. If that's a boy or girl, it will be *mine*," I sneer in her face, getting so close she can feel my hot breath.

"Vera," Logan's tone is a warning. I'm taking a chance being so close to her, but I don't care. There's no way she will kill me if she wants my child. The only thing is, she doesn't realize she's never getting anything from me.

"You're not my mother," I tell her. "You're dead to me. You died when I was a child, and you always will be nothing to me. Nothing you do will ever break me."

"There was no lie. I was going to rule both companies. Your father's, along with the Oakridge name, because Herbert over here couldn't keep his mitts clean. Could you?" she questions, looking over my shoulder at the man whose face has turned ashen with shock.

"Listen to me. I'll fix this," Logan's dad mutters with a hint of worry in his tone. He doesn't look like a man whose life is about to fall to pieces. He looks like he's about to kill my mother and laugh while doing it. There's a burning in his gaze. Rage. Pure, unadulterated fury.

"You've had time to *fix* things for a while now, Herbert," my mother says. "But since you've decided to ignore my demands and burn the contract which took years to get in place . . ." My mother's evil smile lights up her face, and I know nothing good can come of this. "I've called up a few friends," she tells him before stepping back. My gaze locks on the phone in her hand as she presses buttons, but not before Herbert pulls out a gun, pointing it at her.

"If I'm going down," he sneers, "so are you."

Everything happens in slow motion. I scream, feeling the ache in my throat as the sound leaves my mouth. Logan races to the desk in an attempt to grab the weapon from his father, but a shot rings out loudly, deafening me.

I'm forced to the floor by strong hands, a heavy body covers me. My mother's body falls to the floor as she grips her stomach. The door shudders against the wall somewhere behind us as loud voices boom in the background. Clicks, of what I can only assume, are guns, ring out, and men fill the space. The body covering me is soon gone, and I'm tugged to my feet.

Men move toward my mother. They work on her, pressing something to her stomach where blood is gushing from the bullet wound. Logan's arms are around me as he moves me backward, and soon enough, we're out of the office with a man in a suit talking, but I don't hear him.

Everything is muffled, mumbled, as if I'm in a bubble, and everyone else is outside it. My blurry gaze locks on the scene unfolding inside the large, darkened room where I realize paramedics are now working on my mother's body, and I wonder if she'll survive the gunshot.

Not long after, Logan's father is taken out in handcuffs. Before they can escort him down the steps, he stops, looking his son in the eye, and speaks. "I did this for you. To keep you and Vera safe. I didn't have a choice, son." There's an earnest tone to his voice, and I wonder just how long my mother held him hostage.

How is it he didn't kill her long ago?

Was she just that good? I doubt it.

CHAPTER THIRTY-FIVE
Logan

People pass in a blur. Blue, black, and red. All I see are colors, and soon enough, we're taken downstairs. The loud wailing of sirens echoes in the air. The scent of blood hangs heavily around us, invading my nostrils with a metallic scent. The voices of cops and medics echo around us as they do their job.

Questions.

Answers.

More questions.

Frustration burns in my veins. All I want is to take Vera away from here. She doesn't need to go through all this, but I can't move because we need to be here to give our story to the police. When one walks off, another appears.

Two detectives are now questioning Vera about her mother. The woman who left her as a child and never looked back. The same woman who wanted our child because she craved the Oakridge name for herself.

What I don't understand though is why.

I watch my father ride away in the back of a police vehicle, his gaze locked on mine, but I have no way of helping him. Not that I want to. He's finally getting what's coming to him, and he needs to pay his penance. The price of wealth comes at a high cost when you break the rules. And my father's broken far too many in his years.

"Mr. Oakridge," the cop calls, and I realize he's talking to me. I haven't gone by that name for so long it feels foreign to be called it now. "We'd prefer you to stick around for a while. There are a lot of documents in your father's office we'd like to talk through with you."

"I had nothing to do with the company, so I'm not sure—"

"Please." It's not a question. It's his way of telling me not to leave the city. I nod. "Thank you. We'll be in touch. You and your wife can leave now."

I don't correct him. Slipping my hand into Vera's, I tug her along behind me. We make our way to the truck in silence, but the moment we've shut the doors, Vera turns to regard me.

"I don't know how to feel," she whispers, the pain evident in her voice. "She left me, planned to take my future child from me." Her gaze is watery with emotion. "She looked at me like I'm something to barter with rather than her daughter." Her voice cracks and I glance over to see her shoulders shaking. Instinctively, I wrap an arm around her, pulling her into the crook of my body. "She was supposed to be dead."

"Do you want to go to the hospital?" My voice is croaky, but there's no sadness in my tone. The emotion has left me. Our lives have been orchestrated by two people who were meant to keep us safe.

"No." Her response is clear. "We'll hear from the police once they've confirmed what's happened to her." She snuggles closer to me. "Take me home."

I want nothing more than to drive to the cabin. It's far from here, and I'm not sure if the cops would allow it. It's worth a try.

"Wait here," I tell her before opening the door and exiting the truck once more. I find the detective in question and wait for him to finish giving his orders to the men before he turns to me. "Would it be okay to head out to my cabin? It's up in Silver Woods."

He glances at his phone, tapping a few times before he nods. "I don't see that being a problem, as long as you'd be willing to drive back when we need you."

"Not a problem, officer," I tell him before heading back to the vehicle. I need to spend some time alone with Vera. To learn more about her, for her to know more about me. And the only way we're going to do that is by spending time alone.

Being back at the cabin feels different. This time, Vera isn't my prisoner. She's here because she loves me. I still don't know how I got so lucky, but I guess there comes a time in everyone's life where they get a second chance. They don't come around often, but when they do, you make the most of them.

"Are you sure it's okay we're here?" she asks for the millionth time since we left my father's house. I've assured her they'd be in contact if they wanted us back, but we haven't heard anything yet. I've asked Dax to keep his ear to the ground.

We move through the cabin, and I take notice of how much more at home Vera seems as she settles on the sofa. Her legs pulled up against her, she hugs them, but she doesn't cry. I half expected her to bawl her eyes out when we arrived, but she's been strong, and I wonder just how long it will last.

"I loved her, even when I didn't know her," she speaks after a few moments. She doesn't look at me; instead, she stares straight ahead. "All this time, I thought I was the one who was responsible for her being away, even though my father said she died."

"Why would you be responsible?"

"I don't know. Time and again, I wondered, asked, but he never once told me more than I needed to know. It was an accident. She was gone." Her voice lowers to a whisper as I settle in beside her, pulling her into my body. "Strangely, I don't feel sad. I don't feel heartbreak," she tells me. "How can I be so cold?"

"You're not cold at all. She's someone you never knew." It's true. If her mother were around, it would be different, but she never knew the woman. And she's certainly nothing like her. My phone buzzes in my pocket, and I pull it out to find Dax's name flashing at me. I answer, "What's up?"

"Your father's been booked, and they're moving him to the prison to wait for his trial date. Not sure what all they found, but I had my men anonymously send in everything they had as well."

"What about Vera's mother?"

Silence.

"Dax?"

"She didn't make it." My heart jolts. *Shit.* "I'm sorry. Just heard. But they'll want you back for questioning. Apparently, Herbert did right by you and Vera. He claims he was the one who shot her, that you were bystanders visiting while you were in the city."

"So, my father really did want a life for us."

It's not a question, but Dax responds, "Yeah. Looks like the old bastard did actually want what's best for you. They're letting Vera's dad out. Not sure how Herbert managed it, but he got the man released." More silence, and then he says, "Listen, the city is here if you ever want to come back. But I get if you don't. Just have a good life."

"Thank you, man," I tell him honestly. "I appreciate everything you've done."

"Don't mention it." Dax hangs up without another word. And I know I must tell Vera about her mother. And I know I'll have to hold her. I'll have to be there for her. And I also know she's going to have to be strong, which I know she can be.

"What happened?"

"Your mom didn't make it," I admit and pull her closer as her body shakes. "And your dad is coming home." This causes her to shift, her gaze peeking up at me.

"What?"

"My dad said something or did something, but your father will be home," I tell her, and a smile that seems to light the darkest fucking night appears on her face. And I know we'll be okay.

"Thank you, Logan. Thank you for being here." That's all she says before she slides onto my lap, her arms around my neck, and she holds me as if I'm her anchor in a stormy sea.

"I love you so much," I tell her. "Marry me."

The two words slip out before I have time to rethink them. It's not romantic. It's not even me on bended fucking knee. But I always believed I'm no fucking fairytale prince. I'm an asshole, and I'll live it until I die.

Vera pushes away from me, but she doesn't shift off my lap. Her gaze locks on mine. Her full lips are tilted upward, and she sucks the bottom one between her teeth.

"I'm serious. Marry me," I say once more, hoping she's not considering refusing me. If she is, I'll just stalk her ass again. She's not getting rid of me that easily.

"I guess if I have to." Her sass makes my dick hard, and I scoop her into my arms, causing her to squeal. "Where are we going?"

"To christen the bed."

CHAPTER THIRTY-SIX
Vera

IT'S BEEN A WEEK, AND WE STILL HAVEN'T GOTTEN answers. The police have called us back to the city, which is why we find ourselves in the station waiting for someone to tell us what the hell is going on.

"Mr. Oakridge." The detective walks in, looking directly at Logan. He glances my way. "Miss Conried. I'm Detective Moritz." He settles in the chair opposite us. "I wanted to talk to you directly. We found a lot of information about Mr. Herbert Oakridge where Leigh Conried had blackmailed him for several years. However, we noticed that they had been in communication about your relationship since . . . ." He glances down, opening the folder he carried into the office.

Silence hangs between us as he flips through the pages, and tension twists my gut painfully. My mother didn't only want my child. She was planning shit for longer than we anticipated.

"Here it is," the detective says as he pushes the pages over toward us. Logan picks it up, his eyes scanning the page. He hands it to me, and I sit back to take in the information.

Vera Rose Conreid will be wed to Logan Phillip Oakridge at the age of eighteen. Should anything come between their union, we will call reinforcements to ensure they will marry before Vera Rose turns twenty-one. With Leigh Conried's contract signed and dated, Herbert Oakridge agrees to all further points within this document.

If he breaks the agreement in any way, by warning either Logan or Vera, he will forfeit his name, company, and any possessions to Leigh Conried. Once the union takes place, Leigh will be gifted the firstborn of Logan and Vera, to eventually run both Oakridge Incorporated as well as Conried and Associates.

"My mother wanted our child to claim the companies. But why would Herbert give all that up because he got arrested?" I ask, setting the page down. I'm sure there is more where that came from, but I'm sickened by what I've read, and I can't imagine the rest is any better.

"It seems that in your father's confession, Mr. Oakridge," the detective says to Logan, "he wanted to ensure you're never to find each other again. When we questioned him about the contract, he told us he tried to ensure you don't find each other again."

"But he hurt Vera by putting her into a fucking coma," Logan spits in anger. Rage causing his hand to vibrate, and I squeeze it in an attempt to calm him down.

"We asked about that after you mentioned it. He explained that he was trying to force you both to break up mutually. He was convinced that if that happened, you wouldn't *want* to get back together."

"I don't believe he did anything to keep either of us safe," Logan says, and deep down, I agree with him, but it makes sense. If Logan hurt me in any way when I was unconscious, I would've left him. I would've walked away, but what Herbert didn't think about was that Logan was stronger than he anticipated.

"We don't know all the details," Moritz says as he hands Logan a few more pages. "These are his signed confessions. He's also told us about setting up Mr. Conried, which means, Vera, your father, will be released from prison soon."

Tears fill my eyes, but they're not coming from a place of sadness. Instead, I'm happy, I'm relieved, and I can't wait to hold my dad again. He always gave the best hugs, and that's what I need. There's a lot he needs to clear up, but now I know we have time. "Thank you for everything."

"We need to finalize the paperwork. Herbert wants to turn over a new leaf," he tells us. "At least, that's what he's telling us. I don't know all the details because he's been talking to my partner and his lawyer, but I needed to meet with you and give you all the news before you see it in the papers."

"Thank you," Logan says as we all three rise from our seats. "Will I be able to see my father before his court date?"

"I'll see what I can do." The promise is there, but somehow, I don't think Herbert is going to want to see his son. There is so much bad blood, and still, I'm not sure everything makes sense.

"Oh, before you leave," Moritz says, handing me a letter. "This was addressed to you. We found it when searching your mother's apartment. She was living in a semi-permanent rental in the city."

"Thank you." My voice is a whisper. I'm not sure I want to know what's inside. Perhaps she's given me a reason for leaving, but then again, maybe she's written all the lies she could've told me to my face in the letter.

I have a choice.

Do I want to know?

Or do I move forward, putting her behind me?

I've been sitting on the couch staring at the letter for hours. Logan made dinner, we've eaten, and now he's at his desk working on something for Dax while I debate whether I should open the can of worms my mother left me.

"You know you don't have to open it," he tells me from where he's seated.

I glance over at him, smiling at him as he looks at me over his dark-rimmed glasses. "I know. I just . . . it's the unknown that keeps niggling at me. You know?"

"I get it, but don't force yourself to do something that may hurt you." He stands, makes his way over to me, and pulls me to my feet. "I'm here for you. No matter what." Logan presses a kiss to my forehead before he leaves me and heads down the hallway until I'm alone.

I pick up the envelope and rip it open. Pulling out the letter, I unfold it slowly, my fingers trembling. I allow my eyes to scan the page.

Vera Rose,

Growing up in our family, with our name, it was never easy to make a life for yourself because there were certain things expected of you. I learned from a young age to agree, no matter what. My father already had my marriage arranged to Stephen before I could ever tell him I was in love with someone else.

Sadly, I didn't fight. I didn't run. I walked down the aisle, and I was Mrs. Conried before I was ready. My heart craved to be an Oakridge because they had everything. That is until your father came into his own, and suddenly, I was no longer a poor girl married to a man who wasn't anywhere near the upper-class society I craved. But as much as your father tried to give me, I never loved him.

After having you, I thought it would change. I thought I would change. But my heart wasn't in it, and I walked away. I am not a mother. I never claimed to be. What I wanted though, was the name I'd admired for most of my life. When I saw you were in line to claim that last name, I was angry.

I was jealous.

My daughter would have the one thing I always wanted.

I hated you.

I wanted you to pay.

And that's when I knew what I had to do—take your firstborn. I would finally gain the fortune, the name, and everything that came with it. I knew Herbert would leave everything to your child because Logan never wanted that life.

The information about Herbert killing his wife

because she was planning to leave him, along with his embezzlement, wasn't enough. At least that's what I believed. But when I found out, he was running an underground sex trafficking ring for, under eighteens, I knew I had him.

The fear in that man's eyes was nothing short of bliss for me. For years he thought I was nothing more than a whore who spread her legs, but what he didn't realize is, I'm shrewd, and I'm good.

I wanted everything he had. Including a grandchild because I knew you wouldn't forgive me for leaving. But I was blinded, I didn't care, all I wanted was the money, the name, and the respect.

But if you're reading this, I failed.

I made mistakes.

And I don't expect forgiveness; I just needed you to know. You may never understand, and that's okay.

Goodbye, Vera Rose. Take care of the name you're going to gain.

I flip the page around, but there's nothing else. Her final words to me weren't *I love you, darling,* or something like that. Instead, she was more concerned about a fucking name.

I head to the kitchen. Flicking on the gas

burner, I hold the page to the flame and watch it ignite. Slowly, the white page turns black as my past burns away with my thoughts of a mother who might have loved me.

"Are you okay?" Logan asks from behind me.

Once the letter is gone, I turn to regard him. "I'm just fine. Nothing I needed in there anyway. I'm stronger without her, and I realized something," I tell him, stepping into his hold. "I'm nothing like her, and it's the best thing I've come to realize about myself."

And I know it's the truth. I never want to be anything like a woman who could do what she did. One day, when I do have a baby, he or she will know love, happiness, and a family that doesn't forsake you for material things. I'll love that child because it's a part of Logan and me.

"There's something else she said," I whisper, knowing that the confirmation will certainly break him. But he needs to know, to have closure.

"What is it?" His dark eyes burn into me, searing me with more question than he voiced.

"Your mother," I start slowly. "She's... she's

dead, Logan." When I look at him, I see the sadness flit across his handsome, rugged face. And I wrap my arms around him. "I'm so sorry."

"Thank you for telling me," he mumbles into my hair as he buries his face into the crook of my neck. He doesn't want to show me his emotions, and I allow him to hold me as he comes to terms with the news.

We stand together, holding each other up for a long while. Silence is calming as it surrounds us. I'm not sure how much time passes when Logan finally pulls away, cupping my face in his hands and smiles.

"Thank you for being here with me. You're a beauty," Logan says. "And I love you."

"I love you too, my Broken Prince," I tell him as I snuggle into his warmth.

EPILOGUE

Vera

Four months later

MY FATHER LOOKS AT ME LIKE I'M A PRINCESS. Today of all days, I feel like that girl I read about in books when I was a kid. I feel like I'm special, more so than normal because as Dad takes my hand, I take a deep breath and turn to the aisle.

"Make sure I don't faceplant on the carpet," I whisper to him, causing him to chuckle.

"Never, sweet girl," he tells me before leading me to my destiny.

When I was ten years old, I met a boy.

When I was eighteen, I ran away from home because said boy didn't want me.

And now, I'm all grown up, and I'm marrying said boy. He's no longer convinced he's a monster, just a broken man who grew up too quickly. It's what happens when monsters raise us. Logan has come to terms with himself, with his desires and mine over the time we've been together. We're both older, grown up.

By the time I reach Logan, he's become blurry because the tears threatening to spill are sitting on my lashes. The moment I blink, they slowly trickle down my cheeks. Logan takes my hand, bringing my knuckles to his lips.

"You look perfect," he tells me before we turn to the man before us. Words are spoken, but I don't hear them because my heart is thrumming wildly in my ears. It's a rhythm I find solace in for the moment.

As time passes and we turn to each other once more, Logan takes my left hand, lifts it, and places the sleek, golden band on my ring finger.

"There was a long time where I thought marriage was for fools. I believed that finding love was not something I'd ever do because I could never find a woman who would see past the exterior and look deeper. But you, my beauty, did just that."

His voice catches, and I have to swallow back my own emotion, or I'd be a basket case of tears right now. But they'd be happy tears. Definitely happy.

"When you accepted me for who I am—not your knight in shining armor—but your Broken Prince, I knew I'd found my Sleeping Beauty." His words warm my chest, my heart beats against my ribs, and I can't stop the tears from falling now.

"I love you," I whisper.

"I promise you forever." Logan slips the ring all the way to the last knuckle. The golden band sits beside the diamond ring he gave me only a month ago. Even though we're not perfect apart, we've found flawlessness together.

"Logan." His name on my lips feels so natural as I take his hand and slip the thick gold ring onto his finger. "You've taken my wants and needs and made them your own, and I'm so thankful you did. Even though we walked a very strange, long, and winding path to get here, my heart is filled with more love and happiness than I've ever experienced." The ring fits perfectly, and I smile up at him when I say the last few words. "Forever and a day, my Broken Prince."

The priest says his final words, announcing us as husband and wife, and the few guests we have whoop loudly when Logan pulls me in for a kiss. The guys who helped us when we needed it most—Dax, Kael, and Axel—along with their partners are here. My father and Abigail, his friend that has been around a few times over the past few weeks. I'm so happy to see my father has found a friendship that had long since fizzled out because of my mother's wrongdoings.

We don't need much more than this. And there's still one more thing I need to tell Logan, but not here. Our hands lock in a tight hold as we make our way down the aisle and out the doors into the sunshine.

"By the way," I whisper quickly before everyone follows us. "No drinking for me tonight." With a naughty wink, I tug him toward the car that will take us up to the cabin, where we've set out tables for our guests to join us for dinner.

❦

Logan

"You're a bad girl for teasing me," I tell her in the cabin as our new puppy races up the steps behind me as I carry my wife to the bedroom. She wanted a dog, and I got her one. "Prince!" I call out to him, and he stops for a second before bounding onto the bed we bought for him.

"I wasn't teasing," she mumbles, "Merely stating facts."

"You're pregnant, and you waited until after the ceremony to tell me." I set her on the bed, and she compliantly lies back. She waits for me, like always, as I slowly undress her. First her sweater, then the blue sweatpants she was wearing. Soon enough, she's in a pair of panties and her bra, both white and lace.

Looking down at her, I take in her perfectly curvy frame, beautifully smooth skin, and her tits cupped in the soft material, which is making my cock ache. Tonight, we're trying something new.

I reach for the silk ribbons and get to work in binding Vera's wrists to the bed frame. Once they're secure, I move to her ankles and do the same. She's bound, mine, and she's looking at me with mischief in her gaze.

Her breathing slows as her lashes flutter, and she closes her eyes. "I'm ready," she whispers in the low-lit bedroom.

My cock throbs when I see her looking like a perfectly bound Sleeping Beauty. Silence stretches between us, and I move to the bedside once more, picking up the sharp steel blade. With a gentle murmur of, "Don't move," I slice away her underwear, tugging the scraps away from her body, and bring her panties to my nose. "Your pussy smells like dinner and fucking dessert," I tell her as I unbuckle my belt and shove my pants, along with my boxers, down.

Stepping out of my clothes, I move over her, kneeling on the bed between her splayed thighs. "Logan."

"Look at me. I need your eyes on me." It's not what we planned, but something inside me craves her gaze. She opens her eyes, and I take the panties, drape them over my erection, and I stroke myself slowly.

"Logan," Vera gasps in shocked desire. With my other hand, I tease her pussy, finding her wet and needy. Her folds open to me as I slip two fingers inside, feeling her tight heat, and a groan escapes me.

"Do you like watching me jerk off with your pretty panties, Beauty?" I arch a brow at her, and she nods at my question. I continue stroking myself, while finger-fucking Vera. Her hips rise, meeting my thrust, and I can't help but smile at the wet sounds her body is making.

"Logan, please," she whimpers, which only makes me harder. My arousal coats the material, and I tug the scrap of underwear free before bringing it to Vera's nose. She opens her mouth, shocking me, and I slip the bundled panties into her mouth. A smile curls her perfect lips, and I stare at her in awe as she sucks on the wetness.

"Dirty fucking girl," I grit out while teasing her entrance with my cock. Gently, ever so slowly, I slide into her. Feeling her open for me, feeling her accept me, has every nerve in my body alight with need.

Her head falls back, and her eyes roll as I thrust deep in one long movement, and then I still. "Fuck," she mumbles through the material, which I pull from her mouth. "Please, Logan, just fuck me."

Her hands and legs are bound. I'm in control, and I smile as I torture her some more with rolling my hips just enough to give her slight friction where she needs it. I don't fuck her. I make love to her.

I raise up on my knees, still inside her, and untangle the knots at her ankles, bringing her legs up and over my shoulders. Our bodies move in unison as I pull out and enter again. My hands grip the cheeks of her ass, squeezing before I open her. Trailing one hand closer to the tight ring of muscle, I feel her clench because she squeezes the life out of my dick.

"Jesus, Vera, you're going to make me come. Just relax," I murmur, coaxing my index finger around the entrance. She breathes. Her legs start shaking as I move the tip of my finger, slipping it into her ass.

Once again, her cunt pulses wildly, and I

take it as a sign she's nervous. Her eyes are wide, but she doesn't shake her head; doesn't stop me. So I push farther, deeper, and the moment I'm up to my third knuckle, she seems to relax, and I taunt both her holes.

"You're filled with me, Beauty," I tell her. "I'm here inside you with you looking at me as I claim your body."

"I'm yours," she tells me, and I focus on the pleasure, not the fact that she's speaking. All this time, I needed the control rather than her asleep. That sends heat racing through me, and I insert a second finger where the first one worked her over. With my free hand, I tease her clit, circling it, pressing down hard, and pinching it. I alternate while finger-fucking her ass and thrusting into her tight, pulsing heat.

"Oh fuck, Logan!" Her cries bounce off the walls. She's close, so fucking close, but I don't stop. My hands move, my cock thickening inside her, and seconds later, she's gushing over me, wetness drenching me as Vera screams my name.

It doesn't take me long to join her in euphoria. Her cunt sucks me in so deep, I fill her with my seed, and I know that this is the first of many nights I'll keep her awake, claiming her in every way I can.

THE END

DID YOU ENJOY THE FAIRYTALE RETELLING?

Dive into my Crimson Falls duet which is my interpretation of Red Riding Hood... I know you'll just love the Big Bad Wolf!

CHAPTER ONE

Lycan

Life doesn't afford us many chances to make right what we've done wrong.

It also doesn't allow us to apologize to those who have passed—no longer walking this earth. When I was younger, the guilt ate away at me. Inch by inch, my soul was consumed by the incessant culpability taking hold of me, but then I realized— if I allow myself to *feel*, I'll never survive. Instead of allowing sentiment to burrow its way inside me, I've buried what most would call *human emotions*. And all I'm left with is the ice-cold ruthlessness that grips me.

Especially growing up with the family I did. The Shaw name was synonymous with violence and bloodshed, and even though I should walk we're known as people you do not cross. My brother decided to walk away from it all. It hurt at first, but now, I realize family isn't always blood.

Choices are what guide us, taking us through the darkness that's been holding us hostage for so long that when we look up into the light, we don't recognize it. Over the years, I've become accustomed to the shadows, and I've basked in them. I no longer want an escape.

Strolling through my club, Heaven, I stop when I reach the immaculate mahogany bar. I cast a glance over the large, dimly lit space, taking in each patron who has already entered my domain. When I opened this place, it was meant for those who wanted to play, to indulge in fantasies that aren't *normal*, and even though my tastes are eclectic, I didn't realize just how dark some tendencies go. I've learned, though, and I've reveled in the shadows.

Black suede booths curl around silver-legged tables, which seats four people. Each one private as they snake against the far wall. To the left of the bar is the entrance to the club, which is where we've just come from, and I notice how it's hidden by the sleek, black, silken curtains that keep this space private.

Stools line the bar area, and to the right is the hallway, which leads to rooms where the games begin. Once the couples or groups have acquainted themselves and agreed to an evening's festivities, they move to one of the private rooms.

Some like to be watched, so I've ensured that there is space for them as well. Every person who walks into Heaven finds solace, pleasure, and satisfaction. When they leave, it's as if all that happened within these walls are a memory, a happy one, but nothing more than an escape from their harsh reality.

I take in the customers who are settled with drinks. The men in expensive, tailored suits and the beautiful women draped over their arms—eye candy. Most of the politicians and businessmen who frequent Heaven are corrupt, married, or owned by the mafia.

My club offers them a cover for the activities which Heaven is famed for. With Masters and slaves, Dominants and their submissives, along with single women who crave the degradation and humiliation that's usually frowned upon, I've given them somewhere to enjoy their desires.

But everything comes with a price.

Everything.

Membership is not cheap, but there are rules that govern every person who walks in the door, and even after they leave, they know that confidentiality is key. Isaac, the barman who's worked for me for years, slides over a tumbler with deep amber liquid.

"Thanks."

"Busy night?" he asks, knowing that I'll have the headcount before the doors open. I only allow so many people in the club at a time, and each night, I limit the number of patrons who enter Heaven.

"Yes, we have a special party tonight," I tell him before I take a sip of my drink, watching the couples slowly forming as they get to know each other. Each woman who walks in here has signed an agreement that she understands what happens in here stays here. And each man knows that he will immediately cease all play if he is told to stop.

My cell phone buzzes in my pocket, and when I pull it out, I notice a familiar name—Alexei Carnevali. One of the Mafia princes I've known since I was a kid. We grew up together, did shit while studying at university, and now that we each have our own companies, we've become closer than I anticipated.

"Alex," I greet after pressing the phone to my ear. "To what do I owe this honor?"

"I was wondering if you can help me," he starts. "I have a job coming up which I'm certain would interest you." I can hear the excitement in his tone, and I have to admit, my interest is piqued.

"Oh? I'm always open to working with you. Especially if it means bloodshed." I signal for another drink as he chuckles at my response, my gaze landing on the door as two patrons saunter in.

One is an influential politician, the other, someone I've been keeping my eye on. His money has been his downfall, and his wife has no fucking clue about his proclivities.

"There's a convent about two hours outside of Los Angeles, which I need your men to check up on, and since you have connections over there, I figured you'd be the best person to ask. I've heard rumors of the Cartel moving illegal goods into the States, trading them up from the border to the City of Angels."

My ears perk up at his words. "Illegal goods?" I've had connections all over the country, all over the world, but if Alex is coming to me, then this must be big. Even though he must have people down there, I have a feeling this goes deeper than just the Cartel.

"Girls." The one word has me on my feet. My target for the evening is moving toward the booths, a woman on his arm that isn't his wife, and even though my blood is boiling with the need to take him down, what Alex just confessed is more important.

"Send me the info. I'll have them shut down within a few hours. Blood will spill."

"If I were closer, I would ask you to wait for me, but I'm in Italy; a job that needed my attention," he informs me. The lowering of his tone tells me he's not alone.

If he's in Europe, then I wonder where his

familia is. "What about your cousins?" I know the Moretti brothers are based in LA. I've never met them personally, but I've spent enough time with Alex to know they're not men you mess around with.

"They're… indisposed. Miami needed their attention." His voice tinged with mystery has me pondering what they're up to, but I know better than to ask. I don't get into their business, and they don't get into mine.

Nodding to myself, I tell him, "I'll sort this out." The promise is there as I move into my spacious office, drink in one hand, my phone in the other. Kicking the door shut behind me, I settle behind my cherry wood desk. The sleek leather chair molds to my form, and I relax against it before waking my computer with a nudge to the mouse. When the screen lights up, Alex's encrypted email is waiting. "I've got the info; just leave it with me. I'll confirm once the job is done."

"Talk soon." He hangs up before I can say anything more, but there's nothing else I can tell him. I hit dial on Kahn's number. The one man I know will have a vested interest in this.

It takes him two rings before answering. "Mr. Shaw."

"Kahn, I have a job for you and the team. I know you're out on the East Coast right now, but before you dive into training, I'd like you to check out a convent," I tell him, leaning back in my chair, casting my gaze down at the club below.

Silence greets me for a long moment before he responds, "A convent?"

"Alexei Carnevali just called," I inform my best man. "He has it on good authority that illegal goods are being moved from New York to Mexico. The Cartel is involved, but we can't walk into their territory without proof, or we will start a war."

"Goods? As in…?" He allows his words to filter into the silence between us, and each time I think about what Alex told me, the more my blood boils at the thought of what's happening to innocent women.

"Yes."

"I'm on it," Kahn tells me, raw honesty in his tone, but also a hint of the hunter I know him to be. That's why I hired him when he first walked into my club. A man with the desire of a predator and the skill of a trained assassin. *What more could I want?*

"Good. Keep me updated." I hang up, my glare still on the thieving asshole downstairs. Mr. Bardot is nothing more than a cheating scumbag, but he doesn't realize just how he's about to pay me back for walking in when I had to.

A fucking Bardot coming in and ruining shit in my life once more. It's not the first time I've had to learn about their family. The name is synonymous with secrets. The Bardot family come from old money, and with the help of his mother, Grace Bardot, they stole more from us than just a few million.

But then I learned more about Horatio. He's got problems, some than money won't fix. I only found out because I looked into why he spent far too much time in my club. It was then I realized something was amiss.

At first, I thought it was my good for nothing brother, but Darius had no access to funds, not mine anyway. Not Shaw money. But there's more to the story than just the money. The problem is that Horatio has lost a lot more than his livelihood. He's about to lose something far more precious to him.

With a sardonic grin on my face, I push to my feet, button my suit jacket, and make my way down to the main area of the club. Time to speak to Mr. Bardot and ensure that his signature is on the contract before he even thinks of playing in one of my rooms tonight.

Only, he doesn't know just how expensive his *needs* have become.

Available on Amazon!

FIND ME
Online

My exclusive reader group gets news on all up and coming releases, sales, and a chance at early ARC copy giveaways! Join us, we don't bite… hard ;)

Dani's Deviants
www.facebook.com/groups/danisdeviants/

Or sign up for my newsletter and get an exclusive novella not available for purchase anywhere!

https://bit.ly/DaniVIPs

Also find me on Instagram, Pinterest, TikTok, and Facebook under @danireneauthor

ALSO BY
Dani

Stand Alones

Choosing the Hart

Love Beyond Words

Cuffed

Fragile Innocence

Perfectly Flawed

Black Light: Obsessed

Among Ash and Ember

Within Me (Limited Time)

Cursed in Love (collab with Cora Kenborn)

Beautifully Brutal

How the Mind Breaks

Taboo Novellas

Sunshine and the Stalker (collab with K Webster)

His Temptation
Austin's Christmas Shortcake
Crime and Punishment (Newsletter Exclusive)
Tempting Grayson

Crimson Falls Duet
Bitter Vows (Book #1)
Bitter Truths (Book #2)

Devils & Pawns Series
The Devil's Plaything

Author Worlds
Only One Night (Lady Boss Press)
It's Never Easy (Lady Boss Press)
Brazen Bachelor (Cocky Hero World)
Fractured (Salvation Society)
Traction (Driven World)

Gilded Sovereign Series
Cruel War (Book #1)
Volatile Love (Book #2)

Sins of Seven Series
Kneel (Book #1)

Obey (Book #2)
Indulge (Book #3)
Ruthless (Book #4)
Bound (Book #5)
Envy (Book #6)
Vice (Book #7)

<u>The Taken Series</u>
Stolen
Severed

<u>Four Fathers Series</u>
Kingston

<u>Four Sons Series</u>
Brock

<u>Carina Press Novellas</u>
Pierced Ink
Madd Ink

<u>Broken Series</u>
Broken by Desire
Shattered by Love

ABOUT
the Author

Dani is a USA Today Bestselling Author of dark and deviant romance with a seductive edge.

Originally from Cape Town, South Africa, she now lives in the UK with her better half who does all the cooking while she writes all the words. When she's not writing, she can be found binge-watching the latest TV series, or working on graphic design either for herself, or other indie authors.

She enjoys reading books about handsome villains and feisty heroines, mostly dark, always seductive, and sometimes depraved. She has a healthy addiction to tattoos, coffee, and ice cream.

www.danirene.com

info@danirene.com